THE POACHER

'*The Poacher* is another of those poignant studies of rural life which Mr. H. E. Bates manages so extraordinarily well. It is a beautifully told story, with some unforgettable scenes.'

SUNDAY TIMES

H. E. BATES

H. E. Bates

THE POACHER

A Panther Book

THE POACHER

A Panther Book

First published in Great Britain by
Jonathan Cape Ltd.

PRINTING HISTORY

Jonathan Cape Edition	published	1935
	reprinted	1935
New Edition	published	1946
	reprinted	1951
Evensford Edition	published	1953
Panther Edition	published May	1959

Printed in England by Hunt, Barnard & Co., Ltd.,
at the Sign of the Dolphin, Aylesbury, Bucks, and
published by Hamilton & Co. (Stafford) Ltd.,
108, Brompton Road, London. S.W.3.

CONTENTS

To
SAM

PART ONE: YOUTH

CHAPTER I

I

THE wind blew straight up the river valley. It had freshened from the north-east: the direction of the sea. Sudden gusts of rain were coming down with it, light icy rain that was a little heavier than a sea-mist and a little lighter than snow.

Luke Bishop stood on the river-path, staring at the water. The rain was freckling the water-surface finely, and the wind, blowing against the current, startled it here and there into a frenzy of little waves. They were like ripples of dark ice that repeatedly melted and froze and dissolved again into the flow of the stream. Luke stood with his head down. He was quite still. He seemed fascinated by the rain on the water and the endless rippling and smoothing of the soundless little waves.

All the time the river-keeper was watching him. Luke saw it, without moving, from the corner of his eyes. His stare at the water was a mere pretence. He saw in reality neither the river nor the rain, but only the keeper, standing farther upstream, half-concealed by a bush of hawthorn, beyond the bridge. He had been aware of the keeper for some time. Now he wondered if the keeper, in turn, knew that he was aware. And he stood still, a little apprehensive, trying to make up his mind. But the keeper did not stir.

Finally Luke walked on, moving with a casual slouch, turning up his jacket collar with one hand. Along the river, beyond the keeper, a solitary heron had been flapping slowly above the white flocks of seagulls and the shallow patches of flood water. It began to come downstream, flapping heavily into the rain. Luke lifted his head to watch it as though in abrupt alarm, ignoring the keeper altogether.

The trick did not work. The keeper continued to stand

with steadfast patience, hidden by the bush, waiting. The heron passed overhead. Luke turned to watch its flight down the river, his back to the keeper, his eyes on the bird until it had passed from sight. And again when he turned to walk on, the keeper was still there. His very motionlessness was a sort of hostility. Luke continued to walk on, coming to the bridge at last. Once on the bridge he was safe. Lounging on the stone parapet he took up an attitude of sprawling contempt, half-challenging the keeper to move or show himself. But again nothing happened. And now, from the bridge, the keeper looked suddenly ridiculous, the bush no longer hiding him completely, his head bent in discomfort against the increasing rain. Half-taking off his cap Luke pulled it sharply back on his head again with a slick gesture of defiance. A moment later, leaning over the parapet, he saw the dim reflection of both the bush and the keeper in the stream. He spat at them and walked on.

Not hurrying, he walked away up the meadow-lane. The giant sloe-bushes on either side broke the force of rain and wind. He walked on the ridges of cow-path, moving with the same supple slouch as ever, taking three cow-ridges at a single stride. He was a spare youth, tall and rather raw. His arms were long and swung loosely in time with the slouching stride of his legs. His face was bony, the skin sallow, the cheeks hollowed by quick growing. There was something secretive and arrogant in his face, something a bit gipsyish, at once wild and reflective. His eyes, a soft grey, almost melancholy, were very quick, never still, flickering gently in reflection and glancing about and behind him, with almost shifty expectancy, as though he went in perpetual fear of someone following him.

He went up the lane without haste, the rain not troubling him. Once he became stock-still in the cow-track. Something dark had moved across a space of sky above a dip in the low fields. But a moment later he moved on again. It was nothing—a pigeon or jackdaw hastening to catch its flock—and he did not even trouble to follow the flight, his eyes losing in a second their look of alert excitement.

Later, half-way up the lane a herd of cows was slushing down, after milking, their breath foggy in the dim November air, and he stood aside, in the hedgerow, to let them pass. The cowman, squinting against the rain and tapping his sluddered leggings with his cow-stick, halted to speak.

'I count the bums are in again, Bish,' he said.

'Ah?'

'I seed yer mother and the gals carrying the chairs out under the tree.'

'That'll be a change,' Luke said.

He stood in the hedgerow, not moving and unconcerned, smiling a little with the same irony as he spoke, until the last cow with its misty cloud of breath had gone past him and the cowman had followed it. Standing in the hedge, on the right bank, he could see the rain coming like icy vapour out of the colourless horizon. From that point the river-valley looked like a solitary shallow furrow driven by a careless share across a vast flat field, the river a dribble of grey water turning and vanishing into a distance that was flat and almost treeless. Though here and there in the valley odd pollard-willows gleamed like reddish corn on the patches of marshland.

When the cows and the cowman had vanished beyond a twist in the lane Luke walked on again. And turning the last bend in the lane, by the stone walls of the first houses, he came suddenly upon the scene the cowman had stopped to describe.

There, on the patch of grass under the great walnut that overshadowed the house, his mother was piling the odd bits of the family furniture. He grinned to see her emerge from the house bearing a mattress on her head, slithering and staggering with the weight of it as she crossed the wet grass. Now and then she half-turned to swear at some invisible figure in the house behind and to call on the Lord for help a moment later, and the words were so familiar to him that he could have said them for her:

9

'Ah! you damned old skinflint! Wouldn't let me keep me only decent mattress out o' the rain, not you, would you? God love and help us, I did think we'd got through '81 without this again. God love and help us.'

Throwing down the mattress on the deal kitchen table and swearing still at that invisible figure calling on the Lord again a moment later, she stood and re-pinned the hair that the wind and the mattress had tangled across her gipsyish face like a black horse-mane.

Pinning the last strand of hair and lifting her head, she saw Luke. She came across the green to him in a burst of rage and anguish, her red elbows uplifted sharply above her head as though to strike him.

'God A'mighty,' she broke out, 'where've *you* been all day?'

'What's a matter?' he said, soft and ironical. 'What's a matter?'

She too became ironical. 'We ain't out in the street again, are we?' she said. 'Oh! no. Oh! no.'

'Summat afresh,' he said. 'Ain't Dad about?'

'Dad about!' All her fury and impatience broke out again. 'Dad about! I ain't seen your Dad since last night. And don't want. He's just as likely to be in quod somewhere as not.'

'Don't you believe it.'

'Bah!' She began to move away in disgust. 'You're every mite as bad as he is.'

A moment later she was back again. He had not moved and was grinning softly.

'Give me a hand with the bed,' she urged, 'afore I wipe that grin off your face.'

He followed her without speaking, still grinning. And as he listened to her complaining recital about the ways of the Lord and the bums in the house he tried to remember how many times they had been turned into the street that year. But he had given it up before he reached the door.

Stooping to go through the doorway he heard the voices

of his two sisters talking and then laughing together, in soft enjoyment at something, in an upstairs room. The almost empty house echoed forlornly with the sounds. His mother had gone up the bare wooden stairs in haste, two steps at a time, and following her he heard her voice uplifted in angry chastisement:

'Get off that bed! My beds ain't fer you to lounge on. Get off it, I tell you!'

He reached the upstairs landing and went into the room from which her voice was coming.

The room was empty of furniture except for a black iron bed-frame pushed back against the wall. Two men, the bums, were standing awkwardly near the bed, which his mother was already dismantling. She was unscrewing the irons and clattering them down on the bare floorboards with the same angry and increasing emphasis as she put into the words she threw at the men:

'If you were men at all you'd give me a hand. Out of my way. If you won't do nothing don't stop folks as would. God love us and help us, you make my blood boil, you make my blood *boil*!'

'No hurry, missus.'

'No hurry!' She clattered the bed-irons together on the bare boards with fury. 'No hurry!' Her hands made helpless gestures above her head and with her straggling gipsyish hair. Speechless, she seized a bundle of bed-irons and steered her way with them through the bedroom door and downstairs, the irons clanking together with hollow sounds that echoed through the empty house. Half-way down her voice broke out again with its old shrillness and fury:

'And, by God, if you gals don't do something I'll limb ye!'

In the bedroom the two daughters, standing by the window looking over the back-garden with its wintry apple trees and its waste of dark earth, laughed at the sound of her voice.

'Sal don't care,' said a man.

'All the same if Sal did,' said the elder girl.

'Ah! you needn't go. We'll stay with you,' he said.

'What?' she flashed. 'Now the bed's gone?'

The two men laughed, and the girl looked at them with a kind of pitying contempt, her big languorous eyes, very dark, moving slowly up and down, her mouth twisted into an ironical half-smile. The younger sister half-turned and stood with her back to the window, softly scratching her throat with her left hand. There was something aristocratic and challenging in the dark faces of them both, their very indolence arresting and passionate. When they lowered their eyes and lifted them slowly again the two men were caught up in their fascination, but after that slow stare had prolonged itself a moment or two the men would grow inexplicably confused, their eyes flickering, as though they wanted to escape its rich contempt.

Luke began to pack together the remaining bed-irons, taking no notice of the men and his sisters. He could hear his mother's voice upraised in lament to someone on the green outside. One of the bums had some apples in his pockets and began to take them out, one by one, shining their crimson skins on his jacket sleeve.

'Like apple?' he called to the younger sister.

She nodded without ceasing the slow soft scratching of her neck, and without speaking. He chose a bright apple, gave it a last polish on his sleeve and a last look of scrutiny, and then tossed it over to her. She caught it effortlessly in her left hand, against her breast, without a sign of thanks except the sulky flash of her black eyes. She made no effort to begin eating, only turning the apple endlessly round and round with her sallow fingers in its resting-place between her breast and her arm.

'Like apple, Sal?'

'I would,' she said.

He chose an apple, as he had done for the younger girl, polishing it on his sleeve and scrutinizing it in readiness to throw it.

'Don't you know how to give an apple to a lady?' the girl said suddenly.

He half-opened his mouth to speak, but she cut him off, satirically:

'Showing your strength.' She was silent for a moment, her eyes filled with relentless contempt for him. 'Now behave yourself,' she said at last, 'and bring it.'

He walked across the room, meekly, to give her the apple. She stood with her right hand outstretched, half-arrogantly, waiting for it. He put the apple into her hand, trying to smile, but her eyes never lost for a single moment their look of scorn, and he turned away at last humiliated.

Leaning back against the bedroom wall he took out two other apples, one for himself and the other for his mate, and they began eating.

'Ain't my brother good enough?' said Sal.

Luke was unscrewing the last joints of the bedstead and setting the frame against the wall. Humiliated, the bum took out another apple and held it out to him.

'Keep it,' Luke said.

The bum stood in uneasy humility, an apple in each hand, miserable in the arrogant sight of the two girls and their brother.

'That'll teach you to mind your big manners,' said Sal.

By the window the younger girl raised the apple to her lips, rubbing its skin against her own with a curiously maddening languor.

'Manners,' she said in soft contempt.

Her voice stung the bailiff's man with sudden anger.

'I've had enough!' he shouted suddenly. 'Out of here! Get that bed downstairs afore I throw it. Every damn stick out of the house in five minutes or I throw it out!'

He perceived at last that the girls, with the same soft almost surly contempt as before, were laughing at him.

'Yes, you too!' he blustered. 'You too!'

'We've seen you before,' said Sal.

'And you'll see me again!' he warned her.

'Not if I know it.'

She had only to open her mouth to make him ridiculous. And seeing the two sisters laughing at him with their old silent, unperturbed contempt, he burst out wildly:

'Poachers! Nothing but a damn lot o' poachers.'

The words as if by magic brought the mother upstairs again, with scrambling angry steps. She came into the room still trying to pin up her wild hair, her voice challenging the men.

'Who said that about poachers? Who said it?'

'I didn't,' said the other bum.

The two girls broke into soft involuntary laughter and the mother drew herself up against the first man, chastising him with her shrill, ugly, devastating voice:

'Another word about poachers in this house and I'll skin you! Who did you ever see in this house that was a poacher?'

'Everybody knows Buck Bishop,' the man began.

'Buck Bishop!' she said ironically. 'Buck Bishop? I never heerd talk of him. Not once. I know Nathaniel Lucas Bishop. That ain't him perhaps? But not Buck Bishop. I never heerd talk of him in all my born days.'

'Everybody knows—' the bum persisted.

'Do you mean Nathaniel Lucas Bishop,' she flashed, 'or don't you?'

As she waited for her answer the girls began to laugh again, making him a fool, and suddenly he made an angry gesture and gave it up.

'I never meant nothing,' he said.

She had left the room almost before he had spoken, Luke following her a moment later with the bed-frame, clattering downstairs.

The bum, churlish, signalled to the two girls to be gone too. 'Out of it,' he said. 'Come on.'

Almost before he had spoken and before the girls could think of replying the mother was back from the next bedroom, carrying in her hands the family Bible, a great black book with brass clasps and gilded leaves. She came in with the old downright air of indignation, the Bible giving her also a sort of righteous ferocity. The bum began to look uneasy and intimidated before she spoke.

'My gals 'll go when they're ready,' she told him. 'D'ye hear that?'

'It'll be dark before they're ready,' he said.

'Don't fret yourself!' she cried. 'I've got a candle. I ain't in such a state to be gone, if you are.'

'I got orders to—'

'And don't chelp *me*! By God, if I hadn't the Lord's book in my hands!' she cried.

She half-lifted the great book with a swift gesture that made him start away from her. The two girls laughed, aloud this time, richly. The mother made a second gesture of anger with the big Bible, warning him for the last time: 'Ye can thank your damn stars this is the Book of God!' before going out of the empty bedroom and down the already half-dark stairs.

Under the walnut tree Luke had packed the bed-frame with the rest of the furniture and was waiting, undecided what to do, when she came out of the house towards him in the thickening rain.

'Well,' he said, 'what do we do now?'

He was lolling, careless, with his back against the great tree, out of the rain. The casualness of his voice and his attitude maddened her at once. She half-lifted the Bible with the same swift gesture as in the bedroom, as though she would strike him.

'And if you weren't so big,' she said, 'I'd leather *you*!'

They stood looking at each other with brief antagonism. And standing there, in silence, he became for the first time really conscious of the increasing rawness of the thin rain and the darkness. The rain had settled like particles of frost on his mother's black dress and hair and was drifting icily down through the tree's bare branches. He did not need to be told:

'We'll be out here all night, under the tree, if you don't do summat quick.'

He stood trying to think of some suggestion.

'You go up,' she said at last, 'and see your Aunt Hannah. Tell her—'

'That's no good.'

'Will you go up and do as I say and tell her—'

'You can't turn her.'

'You want to argue, don't you?'

'I ain't arguing. It's no use—'

'You want to make me stop out here and get this Bible wet, that's all, don't you? Now will you listen to me for once and go up and tell her—'

They argued briefly there under the tree before her voice grew desperate in its exasperation, and he relented. As he walked away, without a final word, his last sign a shrug of his shoulders, she called after him:

'She's your Dad's own sister and you're own kin to her, tell her that—'

But he had heard the words so often that he did not need to listen. Walking more quickly than before he went up into the town street, keeping close to the houses and the high walls of the big gardens.

Once, hearing sounds, he half-turned and looked back. He could see nothing, but the sounds were repeated again. They were dull thuds of sounds as though his mother, her patience exhausted, were bringing down the Bible, at last, upon someone's head.

Darkness was coming on rapidly and the rain was increasing as he went on, and lights of pub-fires were beginning to flicker up behind the wet windows.

2

As Luke went up the High Street of Nenweald to the town Square, in the falling darkness, walking with unconscious furtiveness, occasionally half-looking backward, as though

16

suspicious of someone following him, he recalled the words his mother had said under the walnut tree: 'I ain't seen your Dad since last night. And don't want.' Reaching the Square, he paused, considering them, making up his mind a moment later to go up into The Bell yard to see if his father were there. He could see the fire in the bar-parlour flickering up behind the lattice-curtains. But going across the Square he recalled in turn some words of his father's: 'If I ain't about, I ain't about. D'ye see? I can take care of myself.' He retraced his steps at once slipping through the back entries behind the old houses of the Square, always half-glancing backward, until he came to the chapel yard where his aunt lived. It was already quite dark, and in the little cul-de-sac the wind tore round and round with bitter force, rattling the iron chapel lamp, the rain like ice. He was glad to be inside the house, in the dark stone passage, holding the door by its big brass knob while he called a greeting:

'Anybody about?'

The strong deep voice of his aunt answered him at once: 'Come in. I thought it was your great slommacking feet.'

He went into the room from which the voice came. His aunt was lighting a candle at the fire, the shadow of her bent body ballooning up across the walls and dying down as the candle-wick caught the flame and petered out again.

'Sit you down,' she said, not turning her back.

He stood awkwardly, waiting. In a moment the candle-flame burned up and she stretched up and set the candlestick on the high mantelpiece above her head.

Turning at last, she found him still standing:

'Ah, sit down,' she urged.

He still stood up. He wanted to tell her his business and have done. 'I ought to be getting back,' he said.

'I'll get a bottle of wine,' she said, 'if you can rest yourself a minute.'

'I ought to be getting back,' he said.

But she had already left the room and was back again, carrying a black wine-bottle and wiping its neck on the hem of her purple underskirt, before he had decided whether to sit down or not. Again, as she reached down the wine-glasses from the cupboard by the fireplace, she urged him to sit down, but he took no notice of her, only repeating the old excuse uneasily: 'I ought to be getting back.' She made tit-tattling sounds of disgust. From the high mantel-piece the yellow candlelight, pouring straight down, made her face seem very like some very old misshapen gourd, the light finding and deepening its infinite cracks and wrinkles and richening the corn-coloured skin. It was a masculine face, the forehead square and dominating, the nose straight and long, the fleshy underlip hanging in a rich sullen pout. Whenever she moved she gave her head a series of rapid shakes, as though in sharp impatience or disapproval of something, her jet ear-rings trembling and flashing on their spidery silver chains like dark elderberries as she did so. Her hair, as black as her ear-rings and as shiny, was plaited into a pigtail that was curled back, almost on the crown of her head, into a thick rosette. When she stood straight up, very tall and momentarily still, she looked extremely handsome and resolute, the endless wrinkles very impressive, the rosette of hair fine and dominating. Now and then she blew her nose with powerful snorts on a large red handkerchief which she kept in the folds of her underskirts, the air sweetish with the snuff she spilt down the silky front of her dress. As she poured out the wine she kept glancing at Luke, very sharply, urging him to sit down again. And finally, when she had given him his wine, he sat down in a chair by the big mahogany table, warming the coldish wine in the cup of his two hands.

The rain pelted as hard as hail on the windows as she, too, sat down on the opposite side of the fire.

'It's a bad night,' he said.

She was half-draining her glass in a single drink as he spoke:

'It's always a bad night,' she said very quickly as she ceased drinking, 'for the rabbits.'

He sat in uneasy silence, not drinking, looking at his

wine and the firelight showing up, a brilliant claret, through the glass. He had sat there too often, bearing a request from his mother for the loan of a pinch of tea or a shilling, loans that he knew would never be repaid, not to feel that she half-knew, already, why he had called to see her.

'The wine's a drop o' good,' he said at last, drinking in order to break the uneasiness of the silence.

'You got the elderberries yourself,' she said.

'Did I? Ah! I remember.'

There was another silence after his voice had ceased, and then her own voice destroying it.

'Don't tell me the bums are in again,' she was saying. 'Don't tell me that tale again.'

He drank and licked the wine uneasily from his lips.

'That's about the drift on it,' he said.

She regarded him in a contemplative silence of disgust, alternately licking her lips and pursuing them, as though to find some word that would fit her displeasure.

'You're a fine lot,' she cried at last.

'I came in to—'

'A bad, poaching, shifty lot,' she went on, relentless and unheeding. 'And I'm almost tired of saying it. A bad, poaching, shifty lot.'

'I was—'

'And a bad, ungrateful lot on top of that!' she went on, raising her voice a little to cry him down. 'And I'm done and finished with you.'

He did not speak.

'What did I tell you last time?' she said.

He had nothing to say.

'You know what I told you,' she said, 'well enough. You know.'

She reached for the wine-bottle with a gesture of angry finality that was a little dramatic, and wrenching out the cork filled up his half-empty glass.

'I was—' he began to say.

'I don't want to hear it,' she said. 'I'm done and finished with you. I don't want to hear it.'

She screwed the cork into the wine-bottle and made it tight with a sharp blow from the palm of her hand. A second later she unscrewed it again and refilled her own glass hastily, making noises of disgust at having forgotten it and then at spilling the wine on the glassy surface of the mahogany table.

'I'm a fool,' she said, wiping away the wine with her handkerchief. 'I'm a fool to sit here and listen to you at all.'

'I told her it was no good,' he began. 'I told her—'

'I know, I know,' she said.

The gentleness and affection she had been keeping back and hiding with her blustering voice escaped at last.

'Drink your wine,' she said, 'while you have the chance.'

He sat back in his chair, at rest, his trouser-legs drying clammily in the heat of the fire. He drank his wine. After a silence she began to talk to him, more gently.

'When did this happen?' she said.

'I don't know,' he said. 'I was along the river—'

'For a change,' she flashed. 'Where was your father?'

'I don't know.'

'I dare say I could tell you,' she said.

He said nothing and she gave up the conversation abruptly. She sat staring into the fire, one hand outstretched, her glass held on her knee by the other. He sat looking at her. He had never got down to the truth about her. There were rumours that she was the bastard child of his father's family. He didn't know. He knew that she had married a well-to-do-farmer who had left her widowed and childless, still a young woman, within a year, and that as long as he had known her she had lived in the house in the chapel yard, surrounded by the heavy farm furniture, the old hunting pictures and the many old books on land-cultivation and horse-doctoring. Time and seclusion had helped to make her a little mysterious. 'You can't bottom her,' his father would say. She could read and write, and had money in the bank at Orcester, five miles up the valley, and also a lawyer there. She drove off to see the lawyer once a month, hiring a trap from The Bell across the Square and driving herself, winter and summer. She wore for the occasion a mannish shooting hat with a pheasant's feather sticking up from the crown, the hat and the feather both askew as if she were drunk. There were, in fact, times when she came home from the lawyer-visits looking as if she had come to blows with him, and Luke had heard stories of mighty arguments on the corn-laws and land-reforms and the church that she would hold over her dinner beer in the Orcester pubs with anyone who happened to be there. It had always been one of her wishes, and was still, that Luke should go into the lawyer's office. But his father would not hear of it. 'God a-mighty, a lawyer?' he said. 'A bloody canker! A liar? I should look well, I think.' And this, for her, was the end of it. Afterwards, when his father, repenting, had gone back to say that he had changed his mind, it was too late, 'No, no,' she said, 'the farther you keep away from the law, Buck Bishop, the better.'

As he sat there, watching her and thinking of her, he thought also of his mother, standing with the derelict furniture under the walnut tree.

He drained his glass. 'Well, this don't get us another shop, does it?' he said.

'What's your hurry?' she said, seeing him rise. 'What's your hurry?'

She was standing up too, holding the wine-bottle, her hand on the cork in invitation.

'If I don't go,' he said, 'she'll be up here after me.'

'Go on then,' she said truculently. 'Go on.'

She reached up to the mantelpiece for the candle to light him to the door, and then, holding it in her hand, half-paused, as though hoping he would change his mind. But he said nothing, deliberately. And she marched off suddenly into the passage, he following her and turning up his jacket collar. She began to murmur something more about 'I'm sick of it, you fair urge me . . .' when she opened the door. The sound of rain rose instantly to a watery thunder and the candle-flame was ripped from the wick like a feeble flag before her hand could guard it. Above the sound of the rain came also another sound, the noise of wheels. 'What the nation's that?' she said. He half-stepped into the rain to look, and down the pebbled chapel yard he could see the drenched figures of his mother and his sisters pushing a hand-cart piled high with furniture. Turning to speak to Aunt Hannah he found her no longer there and above the noise of the rain and the wheels rattling the pebbles he could hear her, back in the room, muttering with a kind of resigned complaint:

'Well, if they're here, they're here, I suppose.'

Late that night, in the bedroom she had given him next his mother and sisters, he stood listening. When he could no longer hear from below all the sounds—the pad of stockinged feet, the sighs, the creak of bed springs, the coughing—of his aunt retiring, he stood stock-still in the darkness of the strange room, waiting. He could feel the silence of the room as though it were tangible. From the soft dribble of eaves and gutters and sound of the wind under the house-thatch he thought the rain had ceased. He stood for a long time, quite motionless. He had turned up his jacket collar and had knotted his black neck-muffler above it. And standing there with his face half-lowered he was as much a part of the darkness as the dribble of raindrops outside was part of the silence.

It was only when he heard at last the approach of foot-steps in the chapel yard that he moved at all. He raised his head. The footsteps came up the yard, paused, turned and retreated again. He listened for a single second longer before going out of the room downstairs and into the street. He moved very quickly. Outside he paused for one moment to listen to the sound of rain dripping from the roof, to the wind roaring westwards, and the retreating footsteps. As he listened the footsteps stopped and then in a moment went on again.

Moving quickly he followed them out of the dark town.

3

Two miles out of the town Buck Bishop halted on the soft grass of the roadside and waited for his son. As his own footsteps ceased Luke's footsteps paused also, but only momentarily, and then came on again. The distance between son and father had kept constant, at about fifty yards, never varying. Only occasionally Luke had paused to listen, his father's footsteps so quiet on the grass that at intervals the sound of them eluded him altogether.

When his father finally halted Luke lost for a moment or two his sense of distance and walked the last ten yards uncertainly, unable to see his father in the intense darkness.

'Are y' there?' he whispered at last.

'God, can't ye keep quiet? I thought it was the thunderin' militia coming up the road.'

His father began to walk on again and Luke followed him. They continued to walk in single file, not speaking. But now they walked more slowly, occasionally halting to listen for a brief moment, but never speaking. The quietness of the big man was amazing. He moved like a black ghost, the extremely soft sound of his light footsteps covered by the sound of rainless wind.

Like this they went on for another mile. Very shortly the road turned to the left, and then at a sharp angle to the right, going downhill. Isolated ash trees broke the level of the roadside; more occasionally still little triangular copses of oak trees. The hedges were stunted. The wind was harsh and stinging as it came unbroken across the bare land.

Very soon they saw odd lights in the hollow beyond them, and for a little longer they kept to the road. Now there were no hedges at all in the roadside. And then, abruptly, Luke's father stopped and stood tense, as though he had heard

23

something. Luke stood still, alert and tense also. Suddenly his father left the road and began walking across the hedgeless land, his feet as soundless on the wet stubble as they had been on the grass.

Luke followed him, saying nothing, at the same unchanging distance as before. The stubble field ended and hedge began again. A narrow green lane ran down a sharp slope from the stubble lane, and uncut hedges of hawthorn meeting each other in the wind overhead. At the foot of the lane, beyond a gate, a light was shining, the window squares orange, the lacy curtain-shadows clear in the darkness. Luke's father pushed open the gate, soundlessly, and they went through, walking quietly past the shadowy shapes of a haystack and an outhouse or two, halting at last under the whitewashed walls of the little public-house.

They stood for a moment by the back door to listen before going in. The wintry branches of two stunted apple trees clapped together with dry sounds in the windy darkness, but there was no other sound except the noise of the wind, roaring far overhead.

In another moment they were inside the warm beer-smelling back parlour of the pub. They closed the door as soundlessly and swiftly behind them as they had closed the gate in the yard outside.

A little woman stood in the room waiting for them, her lips tight, her whole attitude arrested. She continued to stand like that, alert and listening, not attempting to speak or move, until Luke's father had spoken.

'All right,' he said softly.

She left the room at once, coming back in less than a minute with two jugs of beer. She set the beer on the white-scrubbed table where the glass oil lamp stood. The two men took up the beer-jugs and drank, still standing.

While they were drinking the woman left the room again. She came back very shortly with two plates of bread and cheese. The two men were sitting by the fire, relaxed.

'Well?' said Buck. For the first time he spoke normally, his voice above a whisper.

'You're late,' she said.

'Good old Poll,' he said.

He leaned back on the scrubbed settle, sucking the beer softly off his thick black moustache, regarding the little woman with a half-smile of admiration. He was a man, between forty and fifty, in the prime of his strength. Beside the little compact woman and the spare half-developed figure of his son he looked extraordinarily powerful and impressive. His long thick legs, tight in their black trousers, were stretched straight out, the muscles stiff as bone. His coat, a sort of ancient black morning-coat with great tail-pockets, was thrown wide open, and his hands were thrust into the top of his trousers, in an attitude of easy arrogance, the thumbs left free. He had not taken off his hat. It was a curious-shaped bowler, the crown very high and the brim curving deep like a helmet, its blackness softened like the blackness of his jacket-shoulders with the green of age and weather. He wore it on the extreme back of his head, as though he had forgotten it. And as he sat there, relaxed, the old tense attitude of quietness and secrecy seemed foreign to him. He looked so powerful and awkward, sprawled out on the settle, his face already flushed with the fire and the beer, that it seemed as if he could never have stirred a yard without being as conspicuous and noisy as a clumsy bull. But the flesh on his face was tight and fine and his black eyes, even in the half-sleepy droop of admiration at the little woman, never lost their look of watchfulness.

They sat, he and the woman, as though silently challenging one another. Beside him she was pert, like a robin against a crow.

'Well!' he burst out at last, 'what about Bradlaugh, now?'

'Bradlaugh!' She was stung to instant life, her little red face lifted in scorn. 'Bradlaugh. I was ashamed to read it. Ashamed. Bradlaugh!'

He half-sat up, his face glowing at the prospect of argument.

'Let me tell you—' he began.

'You needn't tell me!' Her quick, bird-like voice cut him off with fresh scorn. 'I don't want to hear it.'

'Let me tell you,' he went on, inexorable. 'I've said it times anew, and I'll say it again. No finer man lives in this country to-day. No—'

'An atheist,' she broke in.

'The constitutional right of a country,' he went on, unheeding, 'to enforce any one religion or any religion at all—'

'Religion! I wonder you aren't ashamed to let the words pass your lips.'

'Be damned. I've told you before, Poll Saunders, and I'll tell you again, th' idea o' God is all popery and humbug. Now listen to me. There's no more a God, I tell you, than there is—'

'Then if there's no God,' she said in triumph, 'why do you argue about Him?'

'I don't want to argue,' he said loftily. 'I don't want to argue.'

'Drink your beer then.'

'But when I see you,' he said, shaking his head, 'going about as blind as a bat, at the mercy o' fartin' parsons—'

'Go on, go on,' she said softly.

'Believing all the humbugging tales they like to tell you—'

'What tales?' she broke in quickly. 'What tales?'

'Look,' he said, reaching out for his beer-jug from the table, 'look at that humbugging tale about Moses and the water, the water in the rock. Are you going to tell me—'

'It's not for me,' she said, 'to question the miracles of—'

'Miracles!' He leaned forward, without having taken a drink, to replace his beer-jug on the table. 'You'll be telling me next that Moses in the bull-rushes was a miracle. You'll be—'

'I don't want to hear it,' she declared. 'I don't want to hear it.'

'No, you don't want to hear it,' he cried. 'And why? Because it's right, that's why! It's right!'

'Right or wrong,' she said, 'I don't want to hear it.'

'And another thing—' he began.

No sooner had he begun to speak than she interrupted him again. And they went on arguing for another twenty minutes or more, crying each other down, while Luke watched them and listened. His father was never so happy as when in an argument. Nenweald, like all the towns of the Nen valley, was a shoemaking town and Bishop himself was a shoemaker when he chose to work between his poaching and his long hours of idleness in his favourite bars. And he was great in argument, driving home his points by smashing his hammer down on the bench sending the bright steel tingles and the myriad brass rivets dancing up and down like sparks. And now, refreshed with the argument and the beer, he looked superb, the blood rich in his cheeks, his eye jaunty, the very tilt of his hat spirited and happy, the muscles of his great legs taut with arrogant life.

But abruptly the argument petered out. He was standing up, his beer drained in a single draught. The woman was on her feet, too, expectant. The old tense air, full of alert secrecy, had returned.

'Which way were you going?' the woman said, her voice a whisper again.

Luke was by the door, waiting.

'Sheldrake spinneys,' his father said.

'Sheldrake,' she said. 'That's a fool's place.'

'Why?'

'They were looking for you there last time. You know that.'

'Heard anything?'

'No.'

'That's all right then.'

'But it's a fool's place,' she persisted. 'A fool's place. Everybody knows Sheldrake. You'll do it once too much.'

He was stuffing the remainder of his bread and cheese into his pocket, smiling.

'The day they nail me,' he said, 'I'll start and believe in God.'

'You'll need to!' she flashed.

'Ah!' he said softly. 'I dare say.'

Luke had opened the door, very quietly, and his father and the woman followed him into the dark little passage that led from the parlour to the bar.

'You didn't finish your beer, Luke,' the woman said.

'Go and finish it,' his father ordered. 'Christ, you may be glad o' that. Free beer, too.'

Luke slipped back into the parlour to drain his forgotten beer. In a flash his father was bending over the woman, one arm about her, and she was putting up her soundless lips to be kissed. It was all over in a moment. Before Luke was back from the parlour his father's hand was softly raising the latch of the outer door and the wind was screaming in the gently widening aperture.

'Mind what fool's tricks you're up to,' said the woman. 'And don't forget the key.'

She slipped a little key into Buck Bishop's hand. The door, opened fully a moment later, let in a sudden rush of the cold night air, and the men slipped out into the public-house yard, the old restrained miraculous quietness in all their movements again.

'Be careful at Sheldrake,' the woman warned them finally.

Bishop paused half-way across the yard to call back in a devilish whisper:

'If they're up there we s'll give 'em what Bradlaugh gave the House. And you know what that was.'

There was no answer except the swift, quiet closing of the door. Quite silent, the men walked rapidly across the public-house yard. At the yard-end the half-doors of the stables stood on the catch and Luke held back the doors against the wind while his father entered the stables. He heard the soft shuffling of his father's feet in the hay on the stable floor and then the murmur of his voice reassuring and quietening the horse. Sharp breaths of horse-flesh and horse urine and the fragrance of hay came out to him, the cold night-wind dispersing them in a moment. In less than a minute his father reappeared, carrying the rabbit nets and slipping the ferrets into the tail-pockets of his coat. In less than another minute the stable doors were shut again and the men were hastening out of the yard and away up the slopes of the fields in the unbroken darkness, the light in the public-house behind them already extinguished.

As they hurried in an easterly direction across the dark fields, the quietness of the big man was again amazing and they did not exchange a single word. The land rose sharply, the wind stronger on the higher ground, and it was not until they reached the crest of the rise that they paused at all.

They stood for only a second or two, listening. They could hear nothing but the sound of the wind and the quiet ooze of water filling up the prints their feet had made in the rainy earth.

Going on again, they went over the crest of the hill. Down the slope, to the left, a thick belt of trees cut off the wind. They stood for a moment to listen again, and hearing nothing, they started into the silent activity of unrolling the nets. In the darkness they moved by instinct, never speaking. They unrolled the nets soundlessly, pegging them down by the mere pressure of their thumbs on short ash pegs which Bishop had devised himself. They worked with great rapidity. As soon as the nets were down Luke crouched against the ground and went from one peg to another, on his hands and knees, to test them. His father was ready with the ferrets. He saw the vague whitish blur of their bodies before they vanished into the earth. After the ferrets had vanished there was a curious silence during which the two men crouched like runners. The hush was broken by a sudden madness of sound and motion in the net. It was the first rabbit, in its first wild struggle for escape. In a second Luke had silenced it by seizing the rabbit in his hands. In another moment he had killed it, breaking its neck by striking the skull lightly with his hand. The rabbit gave a single great convulsion of pain and was dead. It was as easy as throwing a ball. The thought flashed across his mind that he could not remember the time when he had not been able to do that. He felt a curious wave of lust and triumph. The thought and the emotion had scarcely passed before another rabbit was beginning its wild struggle in the net.

Twenty minutes later he was unhooking the net-pegs from the ground and folding up the nets. He stood with the nets across his shoulders, listening, while his father recovered the ferrets. The ungutted rabbits lay in a heap at his feet. As he waited he wiped his blood-sticky hands on his trousers, absently. He stood perfectly erect, his head up to catch the slightest sounds. His nerves were tightened like wire. All the time he could hear nothing but his father's soft movements with the ferrets and the distant surge of the wind in the bare spinney trees.

At last the ferrets were recovered. He followed his father down the hill, carrying his share of the rabbits. Their bony skulls knocked against his legs as he stiffened himself against the weight and the incline of the land. Their bodies, ungutted, were a sagging weight in his hands.

Back in the pub-yard, Luke swung back the stable doors and followed his father into the stable. He could just make out the dark still shape of a horse and could hear the soft rustle of hay as his father hid the rabbits in the fodder-loft. He caught the smell of the horse strongly and the stench of ferret-dung and the mild fragrance of hay.

He shut the stable door again in a second or two and followed his father across the yard and through the lane and across the open fields. His father did not once speak. He walked very quickly, but with the same miraculous quietness as ever.

But finally, a mile farther on, at a path in the wood, he halted. He was stuffing into his mouth the bread and cheese the woman had given him in the pub. He stood eating ravenously and listening and for the first time he spoke, his voice thick with the food.

'Make yourself scarce,' he said.

In a moment he had vanished, without a word, and Luke walked on again.

It was not until he came downhill into the town at last that he became conscious for the first time of his extreme weariness. The wind seemed to have increased and was coming bitterly off the river. His hands were still sticky with rabbit-blood and when he opened them to relieve the contraction of his fingers he could scarcely shut them again.

CHAPTER II

I

BY the following spring the Bishops were living in a new house, on the edge of the town, in a block of raw brick houses that overlooked the river. They seemed almost to have settled down.

After the first week or two in the new house they took in a lodger. Bishop, who for a secretive, argumentative man made friends easily, was never really happy unless there was a lodger in the house. From time to time, in one of his favourite bars, he would come upon a stranger to the town, a travelling sawyer or a shoemaker looking for work, and before the stranger could realize it he would find himself accepting Bishop's offer to go home and lodge with him, won over by Bishop's swaggering, generous way of brushing aside all difficulties, of taking it all inevitably and for granted. 'Money? Put that out of your head. Share with us till you're settled. It makes no odds. No odds at all. Some day you'll do the same for me.' He would pay for the stranger's beer and then, at home, would order the womenfolk to set out a meal in welcome, he himself cutting the loaf and the cheese with careless liberality into generous slices. He seemed to take a fancy to raw young men of large physique. It was as though he saw in them his former self, the self of twenty years before. And within a week he would be concerned for their physical welfare. Did they go in for running? Or boxing? If the stranger took no interest in running or boxing Bishop would make it plain, very shortly, that the bed was no longer available, putting the case with the same swaggering liberality as before. 'It's a bit too much for the missus. You know how it is? I wouldn't have had it happen for a sovereign. But you know how women are?' But if the stranger took an interest in running, or boxing an excited change would come over Bishop. He would behave like a man with a prize dog. He would lavish generous compliments on the stranger and, as he sized up the length of his arm or the breadth of his chest, he would remark that he could not help being reminded of Fitzsimmons. 'You've got the build all right. It's only a question of training. A month's training, man, and—ah, you won't know yourself when you look in the glass.'

As soon as possible the training would begin. Bishop's excitement would increase when the training started and he would begin to say that the more he studied the young lodger the more he could see in him the prospect of a national champion. Invariably the lodger would share Luke's bedroom and at five o'clock Luke would hear his father running softly downstairs. A little later he would hear the clank of buckets and the soft splashing of water on the stairs and presently his father would burst into the bedroom, set down two buckets of cold water and drag the lodger out of bed. The lodger, too sleepy to know what was happening or to protest, would let himself be handled like a child. While Bishop shook him and pummelled him into a state of wakefulness Luke would drag a tin bath from beneath the bed, and the lodger, stripped of his shirt, would stand in it with his arms folded miserably about him, like a man in a cold trance. Bishop would then seize a bucket, and standing on the bed, proceed to pour the water over the naked lodger. The man would catch his breath in great gasps

32

of involuntary shock, his hands groping helplessly, his drenched hair blinding his sleepy eyes. Before he could recover Bishop would leap off the bed with amazing agility and seize the second bucket and empty that too over the boxer's head. The man would give out a brief groan of resignation and relief, the last of the water would dribble down his limbs into the bath, and Bishop would force him to come out of the bath and stand on the bedroom floor. On cold spring or winter mornings the boxer would proceed to prance up and down in a sudden affectation of agile pleasure, his hands attacking the air with vague blows. All the time Bishop and Luke would scourge his body with great sweeps of the towel, afterwards slapping it, flat-handed, until the skin was pink and vibrant and the chest-hairs crisp again. Bishop, extremely excited, would talk incessantly in his thick soft voice, giving the boxer advice, encouraging him and warming him with flattery.

While the lodger was dressing, Luke and his father would remove the empty buckets and the bath downstairs. In the kitchen Bishop would make a pot of tea and the three men would each drink a cup of unsweetened tea before going out for the early morning run. 'No sugar! You'll get thirsty enough.' Bishop, between the great gulps of tea, would put on a sort of woollen cardigan sweater, once white, that had turned a strange dirty yellow with age and use. The boxer would be forced to put on a sweater too, and in the early stages of the training a jacket or a top coat, with perhaps a scarf or two also. Then the three men would go out for the morning run. Bishop's enthusiasm and activity would increase as they trotted along the deserted roads, in the sharp early morning air. The boxer would be under a strict penalty of silence, but Bishop would talk as he ran, renewing his advice and flattery and relating stories of great fights he had seen. He never seemed to lose breath or to feel the effects of the long nights of poaching. Back in the house the boxer would be towelled and flesh-gloved down with great care, but Bishop never even troubled to wipe the sweat off his own face. As a young man he had himself been a great fighter, a notorious terror, with a reputation that had never died. And later in the morning he would spar with the lodger in the back paddock of The Griffin in the High Street, showing him the tricks and punches that had made him locally famous. After the sparring the three men would return to the pub and drink beer or stout and argue about politics or fighting, returning home for dinner at midday, the boxer on a diet of underdone steaks. Bishop charged a trifle extra for steaks. 'But nothing to what they're worth to you, see? They'll mean all the difference between love-tapping and a knock-out. You can't beat a steak.' Wherever he went Bishop would be accompanied by a small white terrier-bitch. And something about the contrast between his huge swaggering body and that of the tiny dog seemed incongruous and touching.

During all this there would be no shoemaking. The little workshop at the bottom of the garden would be shut up, its dryish acrid odours of parched leather and wax turning sour and mouldy. Working on the out-door system, fetching his raw materials from the factory and making up the shoes in entirety and drawing his money at piece-time rates, Bishop was his own master. The system gave him utter independence. But what with the poaching and the boxing and odd holidays taken off for fairs and fox-hunting the work he did was almost negligible. Nevertheless he took pride in his craft, his shoes were sound and beautiful, the individual stitches strangely delicate for the work of such large hands.

Mrs. Bishop had no say in the question of work or lodgers. She was at heart a religious woman, slatternly, loud-mouthed, but in reality subordinate. Her life with Bishop was negligible, yet she was secretly ashamed of it covering her shame and keeping her touch with a finer life by going to church on Sunday and little communions and meetings on week nights. All day, during the week, she went about in a sackcloth apron, her gipsyish hair in knots and an old cap of

34

Bishop's hat-pinned on her head. But on Sundays she was a changed woman. Her hair became severe and neat, her manner subdued and almost contemplative. Bishop too was changed on Sundays. He would put on a black suit, a large white dicky and a pair of light brown, squeaky boots. And on summer Sunday evenings after tea he would walk down the garden path to cut himself a buttonhole. He would stand there and gaze at the flowers with a curious tenderness, his hands in his trouser-tops, his large silver watch-chain making two deep loops as he leaned forward to gaze at the sweet-peas or the white stocks or the first dahlias, his favourite flowers. Finally he would unclasp his knife and step tenderly on the earth and cut himself a flower. Back in the house, with the yellow dahlia or the white knot of stock-flowers in his buttonhole, he would call the little white dog and they would go off together. Bishop would walk with a kind of easy solemnity, the little bitch at his heels, and together they would go along the towing path by the river or through the fields of ripening beans and corn. There was something resplendent about him then.

It was April, a little after Easter, when the new lodger arrived. Bishop brought him to the new house in the early afternoon, and the man stood on the doorstep, hesitant, wiping his feet timorously on the door-sack.

'Ah, come in, come in,' said Bishop. 'Come in, man.'

The stranger half-entered the kitchen, his hands fiddling uneasily with the bundle he carried under his arm. He was extremely tall and lean, with large vacuous blue eyes, a mere youth. And seeing the two girls and Mrs. Bishop washing the dishes at the kitchen sink he was terrified. He was half-sidling out of the door when Bishop dragged him back again.

'Ah, come in, man, come in. God a'mighty, you ain't frit at a couple o' gals, I know.'

The youth came back into the kitchen, and the girls, their dress-sleeves rolled up tight above the fine forearms, stood looking at him boldly, without embarrassment.

'This is Jack Reeves,' said Bishop. 'These are my two gals, Sal and Hester.'

The two girls said 'Good afternoon,' but the youth did not speak.

'Let's have a mite o' dinner, missus,' Bishop said, 'quick.'

Mrs. Bishop had not spoken and now she left the dish-washing without a word and proceeded to lay out plates and knives and bread and cheese on the bare kitchen table. Bishop seized a knife and began to cut up the loaf into liberal slices, carelessly.

'And Hester,' he said, 'get off to Maddam's for a drop o' stout. A quart.'

For the first time the young man spoke.

'Not for me,' he said. 'I don't drink.'

Bishop seemed to become embarrassed too.

'Don't what?' he said.

'I don't drink.'

'How's that?' Bishop was beginning to grow uncertain about the lodger's prospects and his voice was half-aggressive.

'I got to keep my weight down,' the youth said.

Bishop's spirits at once returned. His voice took on the old swaggering enthusiasm of tone.

'Weight?' he said eagerly. 'What d'ye do? Fight?'

'I run a bit,' the youth said.

Bishop stood back a pace or two and regarded the young man with cordiality, making soft self-deprecatory sounds at the same time.

'And I never seed it,' he said. 'Never noticed it. And if ever a chap could run you can. Be God, I can see it by the way you stan' still.'

Hester, the younger daughter, had come from the pantry with a blue-and-white quart jug in her hand, her pinafore off, and was waiting to fetch the stout for the men. She stood regarding the lodger, quietly.

'Am I to fetch the stout?' she said.

'When a man's runnin',' said Bishop, 'he don't wanna go guzzling stout, my gal.'

The girl looked at the lodger's thin wrists and face and his altogether overgrown, sallow body.

'That's what he wants, something to feed him up,' she said.

The lodger looked embarrassed again and Bishop began to protest heavily, but the girl looked straight at the lodger and spoke:

'Will you have a drop o' stout if I fetch it?' she said.

'I don't drink,' he said.

'Will you have it if I fetch it?' she insisted. 'It'll do you good.'

'If the boy don't want it, he don't want it!' said Bishop.

He half-raised his voice and the young man flushed miserably, the dark candid stare of the girl and the insistent and almost aristocratic tone of her voice embarrassing him deeply.

'You look about worn out,' she said. 'How far have you come?'

The next moment the lodger began to cough, the short dry spasms of coughing draining the colour from his face, and he could not answer the girl. As he coughed he bent his head, as though to suppress the sound. When the coughing had ceased and he raised his head again Hester had vanished, taking the jug with her.

'Summat went wrong way?' Bishop asked.

'That's about it,' said the youth. His voice was weak and he seemed relieved to sit down, but Bishop, hacking the red cheese into thick triangular slices, scarcely noticed it.

'Make yourself at home,' he said. He gazed in meditation at the youth as they sat eating the bread and cheese, his stare half-troubled, as though he were trying to solve a problem. Finally he half-leapt up from the table in a spasm of sudden excitement.

'Be dalled if I could think who you featured,' he said. 'And now I know. Missus!' He called Mrs. Bishop from the kitchen sink. 'Have a good look at the boy. Now who does he feature!'

'I'm sure I don't know.'

'Ah, woman, look at him, be God, look at him.'

He was extremely excited as she looked the youth up and down.

'He's a good deal like Moll Andrews' boy,' she said at last.

Bishop made a gesture of supreme weariness, of ironical resignation.

'Moll Andrews' boy,' he repeated. 'Moll Andrews!—God a'mighty, where's Luke? He'll know in a minute. Where's Luke?'

'He's in the shop,' she said.

'Moll Andrews' boy,' he went on, ironically. 'Moll Andrews' boy, God a'mighty. Why, woman, any kid could tell you he was the spit of Tim Evans.'

'Evans?' she said vaguely. 'Tim Evans?'

'Evans, woman. Evans! Champion o' the Midlands—the masterpiece of a runner as ever was. Make out you never heard o' Tim Evans!'

He suddenly seemed to ignore Mrs. Bishop and he laid his hand half-tenderly on the lodger's shoulder.

'You get the grub down you—I got a portrait of Evans upstairs. I'll fetch it down.'

'Ah, clomp upstairs,' said Mrs. Bishop. 'Clomp upstairs.'

He made a swift gesture with his elbow upraised and crooked, as though to strike her playfully, and then strode past her with a royal swagger and went upstairs without a word, setting down his feet with deliberate heaviness, as though to mock and infuriate her.

As soon as he was gone and before Mrs. Bishop could speak again Hester had returned with the jug of stout. The lodger, seeing her, was overcome again with the old embarrassment, his face darkening with the sudden rush of blood. Without speaking, the girl set the jug on the table and then fetched a glass from the pantry and poured out a glass of the stout and set it before the lodger.

He hesitated.

'Drink it,' she said.

He sat in a painful agony, as though paralysed by her proximity and her voice and the stare of the three women as they watched him.

'Drink it,' she said. Her voice was soft but inexorable, her very dark eyes never flickering or changing their expression of determination. 'Drink it. Take a good drink.'

Finally he drank. He lifted the glass slowly, seemed to hold his breath for a moment and than drank quickly. The three women watched him. The soft oak-coloured beads of stout clung to his thin moustache and he was too troubled to wipe them away.

'How far have you come?' said Hester.

'Not far. I started from Oxford. I was a tapper.'

'Oxford—that's a long way.'

Before anyone could speak again the youth was caught up in a spasm of coughing. His face, drained of its colour as suddenly as before, seemed extraordinarily thin and frail and exhausted. But it was all over in a moment and as soon as the coughing had ceased he drank eagerly of the stout again.

'That cough's no good to you,' Hester said.

He made a slight movement with his shoulders, as though it did not matter.

'I bin sleeping rough,' he said.

The heavy sound of Bishop's feet on the stairs was renewed and the girl turned away with a slight shrug of her fine shoulders too.

'I thought as much,' she said.

2

The young lodger and Luke shared the back bedroom, sleeping in the same small iron bed. The house had been built on a sharp slope of ground on the edge of the fields running down to the river, and there were two steps down into the little bedroom. On the first nights of that spring Luke, coming home late in the darkness and forgetting the descending steps, would sometimes miss his footing, his stockinged feet slipping on the smooth stair-edge, and the sound would distract the lodger and sometimes even wake him from his heavy sleep. Occasionally when he woke he would turn over and begin his dry coughing, which would go on for perhaps an hour or two, intermittently. It would often be morning before the youths were asleep and it seemed that no sooner were they asleep than Bishop came excitedly upstairs with the water-bucket to wake them again. Reeves, the lodger, would wake in a state of physical fright, as though not quite knowing where he was. Standing naked in the bath he was revealed as even thinner and more sallow than he appeared in his loose clothes. His ribs and shoulder-blades, protruding sharply, made dark shadows on his pallid skin. His legs and thighs were slimmer and finer than a girl's, the hair on them extremely golden and soft. The sudden icy shower of water would make him gasp in agony, and his body, goose-skinned and cold, would seem to shrink to an even greater thinness until Bishop towelled and slapped it to life again. His thinness seemed to both himself and Bishop a great virtue. 'Not an ounce of fat flesh on the boy,' Bishop would exclaim. 'Feel where you like. Feel.' Reeves himself seemed also to think of nothing but keeping down his weight, and the morning bath and the enthusiastic towelling were like the first rites of a religious exercise. And out on the roads in the early summer morning sunshine, it all seemed justified. Reeves, so thin and slight, ran more easily and beautifully than anyone Luke or his father had ever seen. Luke, clad like his father in old trousers and a yellowish sweater, would act as a pace-maker to Reeves, and Bishop would time them with a stop-watch over short distances along the deserted roads.

As the summer came on and the breeding season and the lighter nights made poaching more difficult the Bishops spent more and more time with Reeves, training him for the sports at country fairs in the late summer. It was part of the training to go off for gentle walks along by the river or into the surrounding country, and sometimes they would take the field paths to Swinestead where Mrs. Saunders kept The White Hart. In the early summer sunshine the country was very green and sweet. The land was less stark and barren than the river-valley, trees thicker about the fields and along the little devious roadsides. It was a country that the Bishops knew better than they knew their own hands.

As they walked along, and again as they sat in the parlour of the pub, Luke would sometimes gaze at his father in conscious admiration. In the pub there would be all the old arguments on God and politics, his father refreshed and excited by his own words, the landlady sharp and inexorable. But always, in the end, with the arguments exhausted or put aside for another time, the talk would return to poaching and the keepers. Reeves was a silent man and the walk across the hot fields would seem often to fatigue him. Not drinking, he would sit with his head lolling idly back against the whitewashed wall of the bar, his thin hand stroking the cat, his whole attitude listless and neutral, and when Bishop first introduced him the landlady pursed her lips in doubt.

'He ain't very fat,' she said.

'Fat! He's a runner.'

'He'll need to be.'

He spoke more quietly.

'How's that?'

'And he ain't the only one who's going to need long legs in these parts before so long.'

'Ah!' he said. 'How's that?'

'I thought you were the one,' she said, 'who knew such a 'nation lot.'

He took up his beer with a sudden swagger.

'Don't tell me it's summat about keepers,' he said.

She began to busy herself, silent and tart, with the towel

and glasses behind the bar, holding up the shining glasses to the window-light, ignoring him.

'Well?' he said at last.

'If you don't want to hear, Mr. Bishop, I can't make you.'

'Ah, what is it then,' he condescended, 'what is it?'

'Nothing,' she said, 'nothing. A bit of a tale about the new keepers.'

He was a little interested.

'New keepers? New?' he said. 'What's wrong with Marsh and Willis and that lot?'

'They're finished,' she said. 'A clean sweep.'

He wiped the beer from his lips with the back of his hand, slowly.

'Oh—ah?' he said.

His careless gesture and the languid tone of his surprise incensed her.

'You can oh-ah, Buck Bishop, but—'

'Keepers,' he broke in derisively. 'I never bin nabbed by a keeper yet and ain't likely to be.'

'Don't you be so cocksure of yourself. When this lot—'

'New or old,' he said. 'I don't care who they are.'

She gave it up. But he was curious to know about it all. Why the new keepers? What was wrong with the old crew? He spoke softly, ironically. He would be lost without the old crew. They were like old friends. When did the new lot come in? Familiarity had bred contempt. But in spite of his cocksureness, he was quiet and intent.

'Old Lord Henry is dead,' she told him at last.

'Ah! Sudden?' he said.

'Don't you hear nothing down at Nenweald?' she flashed.

'We got summat else to do besides chatter,' he said, 'about top-notchers.'

'Well, I've told you,' she said, giving it up again. 'Don't say I didn't tell you.'

'What's a'matter?' he said in soft astonishment. 'What's a'matter about a few keepers?'

She leaned across the bar and spoke for the first time earnestly and insistently.

'It ain't going to be safe to *look* at a rabbit round here.'

'Well, I never,' he murmured softly.

'I've seen the new man. He comes in here.'

'Ah! What's *he* like?'

'Big man, fine built. Named Baron.'

'Baron? Ain't his title?' he mocked.

She grew angry again. 'He'd make two of you!' she flashed.

'There!' He picked up his glass, drank the last of his beer and wiped his lips on the back of his hand with the old derisive gesture. 'Well, we'll be getting back.'

'And take my tip,' she said earnestly, 'and stop there for a while.'

'Ah, we'll see,' he promised. 'We'll see.'

But the next morning, even earlier, the three men were back at the pub again. Bishop had a cowslip in his mouth, and chewed the sweet stalk when he spoke.

'You're sharp, ain't you?' said the landlady. 'You're sharp!'

'Let's have th' old trap out,' he said. 'I feel like a quiet drive round.'

'Well, you do as you like, you—'

'God a'mighty, Poll, God a'mighty. What's wrong with a quiet drive round?'

'Nothing, nothing!' she said.

'Buck Bishop can look after—'

'All right, all right. You—'

They continued to argue while Luke harnessed the little black mare to the trap, the little woman afraid beneath an air of resignation, Bishop never changing his tone of soft cocksureness. When they had finished arguing and the mare was ready the three men climbed up into the trap and drove out of the pub-yard, Bishop with the reins lightly in his fingers and his driving hand careless on his knee.

They drove through the village and up the road and

past the last farm into open country without speaking. It was an old maxim of Bishop's that the less they spoke the better. 'Save your breath,' he would say. 'There's no telling when you'll need every morsel on it.' But except on the night excursions he had no sooner made the rule than he was breaking it again, relating some wild tale about his early poaching days or of fights with raw fists on distant spinney-sides on early summer mornings, or of the greatest runner he ever saw in his life. Tiring of the stories or growing ecstatic over them he would often burst into singing. For such a large fleshy man he had a surprisingly delicate, flexible tenor voice. As a boy he had sung in the church choir at Nenweald. 'It was only that shirt rig-out that finished me.' He loved hymns, and the hymns he sang would become mixed with the ballads and pub-songs he had learned in pubs and at fairs. He sang much, but drank little. Once, as a boy of seventeen, Luke swaggered off in the darkness to meet his father from the night's poaching, his legs silly with beer, his head big and proud. He walked with an exaggerated swagger belching his bad breath noisily. Without warning, Bishop raised his fist and knocked him backwards into the hedge on the roadside. 'If you're coming with me,' he said, 'you're coming sober.'

Up on the higher land, above the village, the morning was magnificent. Cowslips had come out in thousands on the grassland, richer and deeper in colour than the May sunlight. In the hollow below, the land, never enclosed, was like a single hedgeless field, vast and rolling. It was guarded on all sides by a circle of woods. Under the woods the slopes were green with grass, but down in the hollow and beyond the village the light emerald of wheatfields was as vivid and sweet as the cowslip-coloured grass in the clear sunshine.

Bishop pulled up the mare at the crest of the hill and let her graze on the roadside grass, and the men looked back over the wide circle of summer country. Coming up the hill Bishop had been telling a story of his early poaching days. It was an old story. But Reeves was a new listener and Bishop, warmed up, kept laying his hand on the young man's arm as he told the tale with the old soft, emphatic derision he kept for religion and keepers. The story was that of a keeper who had followed Bishop, one winter night, for many miles. Bishop could hear the increasing sound of the footsteps behind him and whenever he paused the footsteps paused also. Tired of it at last Bishop waited for the footsteps to come up. At that part of the story he would begin to grow excited, his voice trembling, as he told how he waited for the keeper to arrive and of how he said to him with extreme quietness: 'Don't you think you'd better git back to bed afore your feet git cold?' and of how the keeper turned, without a word, and disappeared.

Luke had heard the story so often that he sat without listening, leaning back over the trap-seat, staring idly over the wide country. His father had come to the point in the story where he was waiting for the keeper to come up when Luke became conscious suddenly of a dog sniffing along the path by the woodside. The air was so still by the wood that he could hear the dog, a setter, panting for breath. The dog sniffed and paused and doubled back repeatedly under the thick green hedge, and as Luke sat watching it a gate clicked along the woodside, the setter bounded back along the path and a man came round the bend in the wood carrying a gun under his arm.

Luke had not time to speak before his father, hearing the click of the gate, had broken off the tale and was looking up too. The man was coming along the path with great strides, but very slowly, his body extremely stiff and erect. He looked like a soldier. He was a gigantic man, taller by an inch or two than Bishop, his thighs tight in his breeches, his large face taut and ripe, the fair skin burnt to a reddish gold by the sun. The big setter seemed like a puppy as it bounded about his thick legs and his gun seemed like a toy under his arm.

'Baron!' said Bishop softly.

'Better hook it.' Luke spoke with his hand over his mouth.

'Keep your mouth shut!'

The three men were silent, waiting for the keeper to come

through the last gate. The setter, squirming under the gate, came bounding across the road, making the mare uneasy. The keeper opened the gate and came through, turning his back on the men as he fastened the catch. From behind he seemed more massive than ever.

As the keeper was shutting the gate Bishop switched the reins a fraction and the mare, startled by the action and the bounding of the setter, backed across the road, her head up, quivering and pricking, and Bishop raised his voice.

'Hey, shopmate.' It was the old shoemakers' greeting. 'Your dog ain't doing this mare no good. Whoa!'

The keeper turned his head.

'You better be getting on wherever you're going then,' he said.

He lowered his head over the gate-catch and finally hooked it up.

'You Mr. Willis?' called Bishop.

The keeper came across the grass from the gate to the road, slow and deliberate. He had a soft fair moustache, almost the colour of his golden skin, that had been freshly clipped, like a soldier's. And standing on the grass he rubbed the tips of his thick fingers softly backwards and forwards across his lips, faintly hostile and superior.

'Willis has finished,' he said.

'Ah? When? When wor that?'

'Willis finished on the last of April.'

'Bless my heart an' life.'

'I'm his lordship's new keeper.'

Bishop made a soft sound of surprise, almost contemptuous. The keeper stood half at a loss, still caressing his moustache, trying to make up his mind about the men. Bishop, waiting for him to speak again, caught sight at that moment of many pheasant coops grouped along the grassland on the south of the wood, and he spoke instead.

'They your bird-coops?' he said.

'They are.'

'Funny place.'

46

The keeper ceased at that moment to caress his moustache and ran his tongue softly over his lips.

'When I want your advice I'll ask for it,' he said.

'Only looks a bit queer to me. You'll get all the south-west rains coming across there, that's all. Willis found that out. Whoa!'

'I thought by the way you spoke you didn't know Willis.'

'Ah, I never. Whoa! I never. Marsh told me. That's how I knowed.'

'Oh!'

The keeper stood for a moment longer regarding the three men as they sat huddled together in the half-ram-shackle trap with their caps slouched and their black neckerchiefs knotted high up their necks. He seemed to come to a decision about them.

'You gyppos keep clear of this estate,' he said.

'What's that?' Bishop half-sprang out of his seat. 'What's you say, be God?'

'I said you gyppos—'

'Gyppos!'

Bishop snatched at the reins as he spoke and the mare, starting forward, took the trap askew across the road. The setter, frightened, set up a great yelping as the trap went past. The keeper took a great stride across the road as though to catch the mare's head and check her, but Bishop eased the reins and let the mare go down the road at a fast pace. Looking back at last, the three men leaned over the trap-seat in an attitude of secure derision. The keeper was standing in the road, his face ablaze with anger, the dog yelping round and round.

'Gyppos!' said Bishop, furious. 'God a'mighty! Gyppos!'

'D'ye think we caught the dog?' said Reeves.

'God a'mighty! Gyppos!'

Bishop snatched at the reins and flicked the mare with a series of sharp slaps across her neck and the trap tore wildly down the hill under the avenue of trees.

'Gyppos!' he kept saying. 'Gyppos!'

His face was furious with anger, the blood very dark under his fine skin. By contrast Reeves had turned very white, the blood drained even out of his hands.

CHAPTER III

I

THAT summer Bishop began to enter Reeves in the running handicaps at the fairs and horse-shows of the surrounding countryside, but the young man was disappointing. He ran as though he were very tired, and Bishop, who had grown fond and hopeful of him, did not understand it and was worried. Reeves' lassitude increased as the summer went on and finally Bishop decided to reduce the morning training and to forbid him to go at night on the poaching expeditions. But Reeves, curiously stubborn and anxious, and above all fearful of losing Bishop's admiration of him as a runner, would not listen. Arguing with Bishop, his face very thin and colourless, his eyes burnt up with fatigue, he was desperate. Where was the sense in not training? Where was the sense? He was all right, he never felt better. And he liked to be out with them on the warm summer nights. What did they take him for? He liked it, he wanted to go! It continued like this until, as the three of them were coming down the hill-slope below Sheldrake wood in the misty half-darkness of a July morning, the keepers surprised them without warning, only the protection of the mist saving them as they scattered. Bishop, old enough and cunning enough to know every spinney and hedge and drain-hole between himself and Nenweald, and all the tricks of doubling and redoubling his tracks and running at an inexhaustible pace, escaped by crossing and recrossing the countryside until the mist dispersed. He was in the kitchen, frying his breakfast bacon and washing the mud from his boots, before six o'clock, and except that his shirt was like a wet cloth with mist and sweat he felt no effects of it all. Half an hour later Luke came in and Bishop fried more bacon and cracked more eggs into the pan while Luke cleaned the mud from his shoes.

'Did you see the boy?' said Bishop. 'Did you see which way he went?'

'I never set eyes on him.'

'He'll be lost, sure enough.'

But before they had finished breakfast Reeves came in. He was exhausted and could not speak. He stood staring at Luke and his father in an extraordinary state of pathetic bewilderment, his mouth opening tremulously and shutting again without a sound.

'Say something, boy! Say something!' Bishop kept saying. 'Where have ye been? Say something. Did they get hold of ye? Say something!'

Before he had finished speaking Reeves looked wildly about him and collapsed. Bishop took him in his arms and undressed him. During the faint Reeves lay flat and stiff on the bed with his eyes wide open and Bishop chafed his wrists with a little brandy, talking to him gently at the same time. 'Come on, now, boy, come on now.' Hearing the commotion and Bishop's entreating voice, the women got up and came along to the little back bedroom. In turn they chafed Reeves' hands and went downstairs for hot water. But, strangely, they asked no questions. And gradually Reeves revived.

From the first he was in a fever. He did not speak much. He would begin to tell what happened in disjointed sentences and then break off, exhausted. Bishop, already reproaching himself, made him a boiling tea of herbs, and that night sat up with him, Luke sleeping on the sofa in the living-room downstairs. The second day Reeves was much worse. The fever was very high, and the women would have had the doctor, but Bishop would not hear of it. He roamed about the meadows that morning and gathered fresh herbs and made Reeves a purging tea, and that night, as Bishop sat by his bedside, Reeves went off into a heavy sleep; it developed into a kind of coma as the night went on and in the morning he did not wake.

Towards the evening of the same day he became worse again and Bishop, alarmed at last, sent Hester for the doctor. While he had gone, Reeves aroused a little and tried to say something to Bishop. Bishop, unable to hear, lifted him up from the pillow in his arms. The words Reeves had tried to utter never came, and before Bishop could do anything the young man was dead.

In the week immediately following Reeves' death Bishop began to behave strangely. Always secretive and extremely cautious and guarded in his speech and often a man of no speech at all in public, he began to go about in a spirit of garrulous defiance. He would tell the story of Baron and the gipsy insult and the story of Reeves and his death over and over again in the bars, always with boasts of revenge. Luke, having to listen not only in the bars but over the dinner-table and on their walks together, grew tired of it all and at last impatient.

'Nothing but talk about Baron and Reeves!' he said at last. 'Who's Baron?—bah!'

'Who's Baron, eh? I'll bloody soon show him who's Baron. D'ye hear? Gyppos!—you heard him say it—gyppos! didn't ye?'

'Give it a rest.'

They were walking together in the summer darkness across the open fields, going towards Sheldrake, and Bishop came to a sudden halt as Luke spoke, and turned upon him with deliberate anger.

'Ain't you satisfied?' he said.

'Satisfied?'

'Ain't you satisfied to let me do as I think fit? Ain't I good enough for you?'

'You want to give that talk about Baron a rest, that's all.'

'I'll give Baron a rest, if that's anything.'

'What good?'

'What good, eh? I'll show you what good. And if you

50

ain't satisfied you be off back. Be off back now! See! You'd be doing a damn sight more good than chelping here.'

Luke turned, almost before his father had finished speaking, and walked across the fields, without a word.

After that Bishop began to go off at night alone. It was the first time they had differed, outright. Half-bored, Luke spent the summer evenings by the river, fishing or laying his eel-lines secretly under the big willow trees, but Bishop, morose and taciturn, never said where he had been and never tried to renew the old relations again, and they kept apart all the summer.

Harvest brought them together again. Every autumn Bishop would negotiate for the work of harvesting from a neighbouring farmer, and towards the middle of August the whole family would go out to the fields, living and working there until the last shock had been carried, the women returning again for the gleaning. In early August, when the corn was in full ear but not yet ripened, Bishop would call at the farmhouse standing beyond the great walnut tree under which the Bishops had once lived. He would ask for Spong, the farmer, and together they would walk through the stack-yard and down the meadow-lane and into the ripening fields of corn. Like a man in a day-dream Bishop would stare across the soft running waves made by the light wind on the delicate white oats or at the heavy wheat ears just beginning to drop with their own weight in the blaze of sunshine. And finally he would run his hands softly among the cornstalks and say:

'What are ye going to give us?'

And Spong would look away over the field too and say that he would give this or that price for reaping and tying, by the field or the acre, with harvest beer thrown in. The price would vary from year to year, with the lightness and fullness of the crop, and after looking away again over the field Bishop would say, 'It's a tidy yield, master,' and Spong would consider it and gaze across the field again and then put a fraction on the price. Then Bishop would consider it and then spit and say, 'The beer ain't good enough,' and after a moment or two in a pretence of thought Spong would name another quart a day. Bishop, satisfied, would gaze for the last time across the ripening field and remark, 'Looks to me oughter be ready about th' eleventh.' Surprised, Spong would say, 'I reckoned not till th' eighteenth, Bish,' but Bishop would shake his head 'I'll be along about th' eleventh, any road,' he would say, and the deal would be over.

The harvest that year was early and by the middle of August the oats were down. The Bishops would be in the field soon after daybreak, Mrs. Bishop bringing the day's food in a shoemaker's truck, wheeling the truck under the hedge on the north side of the field. They began work at once in the morning coolness, Bishop and Luke mowing, the women gathering and binding, the girls making the bonds and their mother binding the sheaves. Except for the noon rest and the mid-morning breakfast and the pauses for drinking the work went on all day, until darkness came. Bishop mowed throughout the day with serene strength, as though tireless, his changeless motions having no effort in them. With the scythe in his hands he was a new man, nothing of the shoemaker or the poacher left about him except his black bowler, which he wore all day as though he had forgotten it. At fixed intervals he stopped to drink; all day a soft beer-coloured sweat stood on his sun-brown arms and face. He mowed in silence: but it was a new silence, an expression of his satisfaction in the sound of his scythe among the harsh cornstalks and in the sight of his swathe lying yellow and beautiful on the stubble behind him.

Luke sensed the change in his father. He felt that Baron and Reeves were forgotten and he was relieved whenever he thought of it. He had already a strong desire to be back in the old way of life: the lazy days, the leisurely walks to the White Hart in the summer mornings, the excitement and solitude of the poaching at nights, the feel of the warm rabbit flesh under his quick hands. One evening as he was dropping his beer bottle on his jacket in the shadow of a shock a young rabbit started out of the standing corn and as it came towards him, running blindly to escape, he dropped flat on his stomach, pinning the rabbit to earth and cracking its neck with almost a single movement of his hands. Getting up and swinging the soft and still warm body of the dead rabbit in his hands, he experienced a sensation of strange elation. And looking across the field he saw that his father, paused in the act of whetting his scythe, was watching him, smiling with the old sardonic approval.

From that moment they were intimate again. It was an intimacy that flowed between them, just as the antagonism had done, with little speech. Looking back into the past weeks of the summer, Luke saw for the first time how dull and unreal the life without his father had been, how little he had enjoyed it, and how much of his life altogether came from his father. As he thought of it he remembered quite suddenly the earliest times when they had gone out together. His father had taught him to set a snare, showing him how to twist the wire to a noose, how to cut the stake and set it, how to cover the gap so that the snare and the stake were part of the hawthorn and the grasses. The elation he had experienced on snaring his first rabbit was the same elation which ran through him in the harvest field. Mingled with it was the pride his father had in him and which he in turn had in his father. It was a pride which it never occurred to either of them to put into words.

But at intervals during the mowing Bishop talked of something else: a new scheme for the coming winter. He wanted to make a change from the old poaching country. There was a flattish, wooded stretch of country to the south of Nenweald, good country, but remote. He had tried it once, many years before. But then the plantations of spruce and pine were still young and were patrolled by keepers and woodmen night and day. In those days it was dangerous country even to him, and he had given it up, but with regret.

He had ever since wanted to try it again. After harvest

53

they would borrow the trap and drive round there and look at the land and consider it. Bishop had an idea that the old family on the estate had broken up and that the big mansion itself was empty. They could find out about it.

During their conversation Luke listened for a repetition of the old talk about Reeves and Baron and revenge, but it never came. He was glad of it, half-prided himself that he was responsible for the new scheme and the new mood. And as the hot days of harvest went by he began to look forward to autumn and the new country.

2

Before the end of October the Bishops began to know the new country very well. They would hire the trap from the White Hart in the early afternoons and travel in a leisurely fashion southward, through the half-strange villages, and along the utterly strange roads running into the heart of the woods. It was a country more richly wooded than ever Bishop remembered it to be: between the old woods of oak and pine the young spruce coppices of his youth had made great growth. There was always a sheltered stillness in the air among the thick spruces, and the sweetness of the spruce-bark would be heavy in the sultry autumn afternoons. The woods, planted so thickly, shut off the wind and the outer world completely, and there were no houses except occasional cottages, whitewashed as though to counteract the shadowiness made by the overhanging trees, with hens running wild in the surrounding undergrowth and across the deserted roads. In the heart of the woods, half-hidden by great avenues of lime and cedar, stood the mansion Bishop had talked about. Catching sight of it occasionally, often by accident, on those autumn afternoons, Bishop would pull up the trap, the little white terrier would stir from its sleepiness in the floor of the trap and leap up on to the seat, and Bishop would smooth his hand absently backwards and forwards across the dog's head as he gazed at the house and pointed out its features. It was the windows and the chimneys of the place that interested Bishop. 'Never a mossel o' smoke, see? Not a mossel. And the shutters all up. D'ye twig it?' As they drew up by the wall of the park one afternoon the rustle of the horse's feet in the fresh-fallen leaves startled a multitude of rabbits in the deserted park such as they had never seen. When the rabbits had vanished nothing moved across the whole space of that quiet parkland except the falling leaves of beech and lime. Bishop drove on in a silence, almost a stupor, of wonder. In all their wanderings up and down the woodlands and about the park they had never seen a keeper: only a solitary woodman, very old, cutting up a fallen beech with feeble blows of an axe. The place seemed altogether forgotten and lost in the profound solitude. Bishop halted the trap on another afternoon and alighted and tried each of the five high iron gates, crested with a shield of blue and gold, as they came to them. The locks were fast and stiff with rust from the summer rains, and drifts of poppy and grass and marigold had seeded themselves in the carriage drives curving away under the trees.

'You could lay your nets in broad daylight,' Bishop marvelled.

But still he was faintly suspicious. It was not enough that he should see the place forgotten and deserted by day. He wanted also to see it and make a safe trespass across it by night.

'We ain't th' only chaps with a couple o' ferrets and a net. And I ain't sure about keepers yet. When I was a boy-chap this park was lousy with keepers.'

They watched for signs of keepers wherever they went: a mole-trap set across a pathway in the woods, the dead skins of stoat and weasel and jay and magpie strung up on the edges of the ridings. But they saw nothing. Instead, in the autumn stillness, they would hear the squawk and cackle of prey-birds hidden in the great trees or flying across the deserted parkland. Seeing one afternoon a weasel taking the thin train of her young across the road, Luke drawled:

'You ain't going to tell me there's keepers in this place—not after that?'

'What's a weasel or two?' said Bishop. 'What's a weasel or two in a place this size? We'll keep quiet a bit.'

Towards the end of October they kept away from the place for about a week. It was soft autumn weather, the days still and sunny, the nights warm and heavy with dew, and in the peaceful unoccupied afternoons Luke would loll by the river, in some secluded place brooded over by a hawthorn that had not lost its leaves, with a sly line at rest in the quiet water. The old training runs in the early mornings had broken off with Reeves' death and had not been renewed; but the long habit itself could not be broken, and he would be out in the early morning, alone or with Bishop, the same as ever, coming home to breakfast with a neckerchief of mushrooms or his eels strung on a reed.

There was a half-monotonous pleasure in the easy days that left him languid. During the summer he had grown thinner and taller. The harvest had been good and the Bishops were well off, but the work had tried him. He was glad of the easy days and the quiet weather that were like balm on his own lassitude. That autumn, thinking of the new poaching schemes, he did not once go to see his aunt Hannah. He had no desire for anything but the soft quiet days. And living that purely physical life, he never thought of the future except in terms of the deserted park and the house standing among its limes and cedars in the heart of the woodland. He never paused to think whether he cared if life ever went farther than that. He wanted only to take the dreamy physical days as they came and then forget them when they had gone.

With part of the harvest-money Bishop had bought three new nets. Beyond that he would not go. They would wait a little—they could afford to wait. And after the languid uneventful days they would pass the evenings in one or other of his favourite bars. Bishop often argued so intensely over God and Bradlaugh that Luke would sit and listen in a kind of alarmed suspense, half-afraid that his father had forgotten what they had planned to do.

And seeing him one evening sitting like that, suspended and silent, the landlady remarked:

'Luke ain't in trouble, Bish, is he?'

'He don't know what trouble is,' said Bishop.

'Ain't gals, is it?'

'Gals!' said Bishop. 'He's got summat more important to trouble his head about than gals.'

3

A clock was striking nine somewhere as they climbed over the wall of the park, early in November, on a night of warm darkness. The rains of autumn had been slight and the turf below the wall was soft but dry, taking the weight of their jumps silently. They had chosen a place where there was a gap between the trees, and in the clear starlight they could see the park stretching out before them with perfect clearness, into the black distance of cedars and leafless limes. They paused for a moment under the wall to listen, but the night seemed soundless. It was only when they began to move again that its sounds awoke: the scuffle of an odd rabbit or two into hiding, the flutter of disturbed wings in the dark branches and the sound of their feet rustling invisible leaves.

The first sounds brought them to a sudden standstill again, listening. They did not speak. They were sounds which normally they would have dismissed unconsciously, as part of the silence and the darkness, but in a strange place the sounds too were strange, and they stood for a moment arrested in half-alarm before walking on again. They had walked the ten miles from Nenweald under cover of darkness, by the little by-roads, missing the villages, bringing nothing with them except an ash stick, a mouthful of bread and cheese which they had already eaten as they walked along. Bishop had decided that they might enter the park on the south side and cross it diagonally, going north-wards, making an exploration.

Out in the park, in the unbroken space of grassland between the thick belt of trees and the mansion itself the night was utterly silent. The feet of the men were soundless. They were walking now, due northward, the stars by the Plough very brilliant to the right of the great house, the Plough half-inverted. Before them, high above its stone terraces, beyond the cedar trees, the house had a look of strange remoteness. In the clear starlight the many white closed shutters of the windows were just visible, the pale stone face of the house broken up horizontally here and there by the blackness of the slender cedar branches. There were no lights and no sound of life except as they drew nearer to the place the quiet sound of running water—the sound of a waterfall flowing invisibly down somewhere beyond the cedars and the terraces. The water itself flowed away into a thin stream across the park and as they crossed the stream in a single leap Luke caught the smell of the water, half-sweet, half-rotten with the odour of fallen leaves. Soon after they had crossed the stream they came to a halt again under the first of the balustraded terraces. And standing there, motion-less, they could hear nothing again but the constant flow of the waterfall. They stood for a long time listening. But except for the sound of water and the light of the stars it was as if they were in a remote and lifeless world.

They walked on again at a sign from Bishop. Crossing what had once been the great lawn between the cedar trees and the terraces they could feel the uncut grass thick and rank under their feet, and Luke came upon a sprinkling of mushrooms, strangely white in the dark grass. But opening his knife and stooping to cut them he suddenly paused and called to Bishop.

'Here,' he whispered. 'Look.'

Bishop bent silently over the mushrooms. Then he ran his hands among them. Between the young fresh buttons that had sprung up that day the thick stalks of the old had

58

been cut off. He picked up a severed stalk in his hand. He fingered the clean knife-cut and squeezed the stalk until a thin juice, like dew, came out on his fingers.

'Ain't been so long, either,' he said.

Luke shut up his knife and Bishop rose, and they went on together across the lawn without touching the mushrooms. They were beyond the terraces, in rough grassland, before Bishop spoke again.

'We're second,' he said, and then, before Luke could answer, he whispered for him to listen.

Listening, Luke could hear nothing but the sudden intermittent flap of an owl flying somewhere in the direction of the house. A moment later the sounds came nearer and the owl, flying very low, wandered dimly over the terraces and then out of hearing. They stood there listening for it to return, but it did not come and finally they moved on again, Bishop very quiet and with an air of caution, as though he were still not satisfied.

They walked across the parkland on the far side of the house without once looking back and without once hearing another sound. The sound of the waterfall had faded away, the owl had not returned, and it was only when they reached a point where the thick woods of spruce came down to the edge of the park that they began to hear sounds again—the old sounds of rabbits scuffling, of disturbed wings in the wood, and the faint noises of fallen leaves.

The air was filled with nothing but the perpetual sweetness of spruce-bark. Falling heavily, it smothered the mellowness of the autumn grass. The trees themselves were still, moving less than the stars that winked and trembled beyond their fragile branches, and under their shadow the old sense of lifelessness returned.

It was all as they had hoped and wanted, and coming presently to a gate they climbed into the wood, walking up one riding and down another without hearing anything but the old sounds of birds and leaves.

Under the trees the darkness was intense. The stars were

59

thinned to mere solitary flashes by the blackness and thickness of spruce branches. And coming down the last of the ridings towards the open parkland they were not conscious of the dark figure standing by the fence until they were twenty yards away.

They stood stock-still, watching him. In the thick wood-darkness they could feel him watching them in return. They stood like that, motionless and watchful, for fully a minute without seeing him stir and without themselves moving or even whispering.

Then Bishop began to retreat, step by step, in utter silence in the rank wood-grass, moving backwards. Then Luke began to retreat. It was an old ruse and had often succeeded. He felt at that moment quite calm, filled with a kind of sober expectancy which increased at each of his backward steps. He watched the figure by the stile with the same increasing expectancy, wondering when he would move and why he did not move. And as the minutes went past and the distance of their retreat increased he began to feel a kind of contempt for him and a kind of exultation in himself.

They had retreated twenty or thirty yards and the figure by the fence had become almost a part of the darkness again when Bishop began to run. He turned quite suddenly, without a sign, and began to run with long silent strides down the riding.

Luke turned and began to run also, a little faster. He had always admired the ease and strength of Bishop's running, and he was already half-consciously lost in admiration of his smooth unvarying pace when a gunshot went off behind him, the shot tearing wildly past him into the darkness.

He began to run at a great pace down the riding as soon as the shot was fired, like a man moving off at the gun-signal in a race. Behind him he could hear the approaching sounds of other feet and before him the sound of Bishop's long easy stride going on as steadily as though the shot had never been fired. As he passed his father his admiration at that stride turned partly to fear and partly to anger. He expected every moment to hear the sound of another shot. He muttered a word or two of impatience as he went past his father, but Bishop did not answer and did not increase his pace, and to his surprise the shot did not come.

He vaulted the fence at the riding-end with a great leap. A minute later, as he set off across the park, he heard the scrape of Bishop's boot-nails on the fence slats as he climbed the fence. He half-turned to shout his impatience again when the second shot was fired. The sound, tearing through the confined space among the spruces, was so near and so terrific that it made him stagger. In his half-turned attitude he thought he saw Bishop stagger too. He half-stopped. He could hear Bishop panting heavily. Beyond him, in the wood, the sounds of pursuit had suddenly ceased. Before they were renewed again Bishop had caught up with him, running with the same old easy and unchanging stride.

They began to run diagonally across the park, away from the house, taking a northerly direction almost unconsciously. They were running together now. 'All right?' Luke asked. Bishop did not answer him. He had a momentary fear that his father had been hit by the shot, but it passed, his old admiration at the strong smooth stride returning instead again. That, too, vanished as he heard the sound of feet again and the brief crack of the wooden gunstock striking the fence slats.

From these sounds he knew that they had a start of forty or fifty yards. He knew that it was enough, and a feeling of sharp surprise shot through him as he first became aware of Bishop increasing his pace.

Nevertheless he increased his own pace also. His confidence in his father at that moment took the form of an excited exultation. Whatever he did was safe; whatever he did was surprisingly right. The exultation gave him fresh strength, a kind of contemptuous courage. He did not care what might happen. The steadiness of the sounds of pursuit behind him did not matter.

Gradually the heavy fragrance of spruce-bark diminished

and faded away. The park, after the intense blackness of the woods, seemed dangerously light under the clear starlight. It began to seem of vast extent also. They seemed already to have been running for many miles and during many hours.

He was running now on his second wind and the sweat was beginning to come out on his face. The sounds behind them had already diminished and long before the wall of the park appeared before them in the darkness they had ceased altogether. Without them the night silence seemed illimitable. There was something also ominous about it too.

Until they reached the wall it was broken only by the sound of their own feet in the grass and by the noise of Bishop spitting and snorting at intervals as he renewed his breath. At the wall they awoke again the rustle of dead leaves under the belt of trees, the flutter and scuffle of odd rabbits and birds. Once they were on the other side of the wall they, too, were silent.

Out on the road Bishop ran on implacably, turning to the right without pausing. He had reverted now to the old pace. The stars of the Plough lay half-over on the left hand of the men, very bright through the half-bare tree branches spreading and meeting over the little road. Under the trees it was very warm, the air damp and sultry as if with summer thunder. The men ran without speaking, one behind another, Bishop leading, always on the roadside grass.

They ran on thus for a great distance, leaving the first road for a second and that in turn for another and then another, forking and zigzagging through the belts of spruce and pine without pausing or speaking or changing their pace, the North Star always in front of them. There became no question any longer of pursuit. Running, Luke half-forgot the park, the wood, the sudden shots tearing through the trees and the succeeding pursuit of feet.

He was glad when his father stopped at last, dropping suddenly down, without warning, on the grassy slope of a stream going under the road.

'Hold hard,' said Bishop.

He was glad to hear his father's voice, thick but not breathless. Dropping down beside him he half-lay on the autumn-wet grass, panting, spitting a little to clear his mouth. He could hear, as he had done in the park, the faint trickle of water: a little stream coming down from the quiet fields over a bed of stones. He lay listening to it until his father's voice broke the stillness again.

'Here, feel that.'

Bishop had rolled up the right leg of his trousers. 'Feel that,' he said again. He was running his hand down his bared leg. Luke, too, put his hand on the bare flesh, feeling the coarse hairs and the sweat-warm skin.

There was a warm stickiness of congealing blood on his hand when he drew it away. 'Christ!' he said. Mechanically he wiped his hand in the grass.

'Shot?' he said.

'I felt it catch me,' said Bishop.

'Where'd it catch you?'

'It ain't much,' said Bishop. 'The blood's dry a'ready. It's dry a'ready.'

'Are y'all right?'

'Wind a minute, that's all. Wind a minute.'

They lay for what seemed a long time on the grass. The sweat dried cold on their limbs. The coolness from the brook rose up and fell like dew. Luke could hear his father panting quickly in the recovery of his breath and except for the quiet ripple of the stream there was no other sound.

'What clock is it, d'ye reckon?' Bishop said at last.

'Ten or more. Where are we?'

'We're all right,' murmured Bishop. 'We're all right.'

Bishop rose as he spoke and almost simultaneously Luke rose too. His father's words gave him an immense assurance. It continued with him long after they had risen from the brookside and had proceeded onwards along the dark maze of roads between the darker woods.

They were walking now. Their sense of distance and place had grown a little confused, so that Bishop paused sometimes to deliberate at the road-crossings. They seemed to be going on for ever through illimitably dark strange country, nothing except a disturbed bird or leaf and themselves moving.

Once or twice Luke spoke of the shot: 'Where'd it hit ye? How d'ye feel?' Until finally Bishop turned on him with impatience:

'God a'mighty, keep on about that shot. Keep on. Ye might think I'd been hit be a damn cannon-ball.'

After that they went on in silence, walking at a regular easy pace, Bishop never pausing or slackening.

It was only when they began to leave the woods behind at last and came into the more open country of the first fields and the first solitary farms that Bishop seemed to grow suddenly tired. He began to walk more slowly. Simultaneously Luke could hear his breath indrawn heavily and expelled again with a sharp gasp as though of pain. But he said nothing, and Luke, remembering his last words, kept silent too.

They were still in strange country, a country still patched with odd copses of spruce between the farms, when Bishop sank down on the grass again for the first of many pauses. In one of these sudden and involuntary pauses they had been resting for fully a minute on the roadside grass before Luke became aware that they were lying under the garden-hedge of a farmhouse standing a little back from the road, a low yellow-washed house half-hidden by its own stacks and overhead trees.

He had hardly realized it when, somewhere behind the stacks and the cluster of cow hovels, a dog began barking. It began to bark first in anger and then with intermittent howls at the scent of their presence. The sounds echoed loudly over the quiet land. He sprang up, wildly, startled for the first time that night into fear. He could hear the running jingle of the dog chain as the dog leapt to escape. And he saw for the first time a light in the window of the farmhouse.

Seeing the light, he urged his father. 'Come on, come on!' but to his astonishment Bishop did not move. He bent down to him half in anger. And again, hearing the dog break into a fresh frenzy of barking and howling, he urged his father to come.

'All of a damn sweat, ain't you?' His father's voice was quiet and unperturbed. But he did not rise.

The light in the house was moving now, going from window to window, and finally Luke could see the yellow glow of a candle held close against the glass of a window by the door. As he made another appeal to his father to get up, standing over him in helplessness and danger, the dog barking more wildly than ever, the candle was drawn away from the window. When it had gone the darkness seemed more intense than ever. He saw nevertheless that his father was getting up. And half-putting his arms about him he made as though to help him to his feet, but with an immense effort Bishop shook him off and with a great stagger up-righted himself.

The door of the farmhouse opened suddenly as he stood there. Held low in the doorway, the candle threw its light full across the dark garden, the long shadows of the old fruit trees reaching slenderly to the road and the field beyond. As though seeing the light the dog began to tear at its chain with fresh terror, and a high voice, the voice of a woman, was raised to quieten it:

'Rouser, be quiet, be quiet! Will you be quiet?'

Finally, when the dog had quietened momentarily, only whimpering in suppressed panic on its dribbling chain, the voice called into the garden:

'Who's there? Who is it? Who's there?'

As the voice called again Bishop began to run, without warning, at the old strong easy stride, as he had done in the wood. In the second or two before following him Luke saw with strange clearness a young woman in the doorway of the farmhouse: her arrested attitude of alarm, the candle fluttering in her hands, her light hair turned lighter still at its soft edges by the near candlelight. He saw it all in a single moment with unforgettable clarity before he, too, began to run and the old thick hedge of hawthorn came between himself and the house, shutting off the yellow-washed walls, the slender trees half-illuminated with candlelight, and lastly, the candlelight and the girl herself.

They went on after that with constantly increasing pauses during which Bishop half-crouched on the ground on one knee, like a runner resting before a race. He never spoke except to answer the questions Luke put to him, his tone sharp and impatient. Finally he burst out: 'Ah, shut up about it, shut up. Ain't I told ye I'm all right? Ain't I told ye?'

They came to the familiar country about Nenweald in the early morning. It was almost two o'clock by the clock in the kitchen when they slipped into the house. Bishop sat down in the high-slatted wooden chair by the empty fireplace. Then in the darkness Luke took off his own boots. The little white terrier, half-asleep under the table woke to life as they came in and Bishop called her to him as he sat in the chair and she sprang softly up to him and lay in his lap. As the bitch leapt against him he gave a sudden exclamation of pain. The dog whimpered a little and Bishop quietened her: 'Good gal, lay still, lay still.'

Luke stood with his boots in his hand, in the darkness, waiting.

'You git off,' Bishop said.

'Ain't you coming?'

'You git off.'

It was the old relentless stubbornness of tone. Without waiting or speaking another word Luke opened the stairs door and went up the wooden stairs soundlessly in his stockinged feet, the motion of climbing the steps draining his strength more than all the long running in the darkness had done.

When he came down again in the morning his father was still sitting there, as he had left him, with the dog on his knees. His boots were half-unlaced, as though he had tried to take them off, and the buttons of his trousers were undone, showing the thickness of congealed blood on his shirt where the shot had entered the groin.

The dog had fallen asleep on his knees, and Bishop's head hung stiffly down on his chest as though he had fallen asleep too.

4

The death of his father robbed him of all spirit. He stood helpless among sudden complexities. His aunt lent him a black suit of her late husband's for the funeral and he wore it as though in a dream, moving about lifelessly, feeling nothing, only an eternal deadness of spirit and thought. Like the suit, his grief seemed to have been borrowed for the occasion. He stood suspended in a strange world that belonged neither to the past nor the future; the past too painful to remember, the future having no meaning for him. After the funeral, in the evening, he went in response to an invitation that was almost like a command to see his aunt; and while she talked to him he sat by the table, as he had done so often, wine-glass in hand, and stared at the fire shining up through the red wine. Listening with the same unalterable deadness of spirit that even the wine could not drive away, he knew only half what she said. She, too, was in black and she looked like the black ghost of her former self, only the inexorable quality of her voice unchanged.

He scarcely uttered a word. She was talking of the future, never mentioning either the past or his father, as though they had died with one another. Though she did not mention it he knew that she expected him to give up the old life, and the spirit of resistance was so deadened in him that he was ready to surrender to whatever she asked. He had not the heart to argue with her. 'It don't matter a sight, one way or another,' he kept thinking.

She was talking of the lawyer's office again and her words took on a level, phlegmatic tone. They came to her lips easily, as though she had long since made up her mind what she wanted to say. She seemed also to have taken for granted his own reception of them. 'And then if you get on, and there's no reason why you shouldn't, they might take you into partnership. You know what that would mean?' Listening unconsciously, he did not answer her question, and as though to reassure him she said, 'I'll see that your mother don't come to want.' He nodded at that and she resumed the steady recital of her ambitions for him, painting the future a favourable rose, just as the fire pinked the silky blackness of her funeral dress.

Finally, as she filled up his glass for the last time, she asked him for the first time what he thought of it all.

'I don't want to hurry you,' she said.

'I was going to say, I'd like to think it over.'

'That's it,' she said. 'You think it over.'

'I ain't much of a writer,' he said. 'Neither a speller, come to that.'

'Worse heads than yourn have got over that.'

'Soon as I get a pen in my hands I feel all buck-fisted, some-how.'

'Your dad was a good writer,' she said.

'Ah, he wor that. He never learnt me, though.'

'You couldn't expect him,' she flashed, 'to teach you every mortal thing.'

The inference in her words was lost on him. He went away with the same deadness of spirit as he had come, promising to think it over, to come back one evening and let her know.

But as he mooned about the meadows in the early November days he could not make up his mind and his old assurance did not return. The mushrooms were finished and towards the end of November the quiet weather broke up. The long rains flooded the meadows and bared the last of the trees. Indoors, in the little tapping-shed at the end of the garden, he sat and worked at his last, the rain penning him there all day. For the first time in his life he became conscious of the emotion of complete unhappiness. Having lived a physical life for so long he did not know what to do with a life filled with such emotion and such quietness now that it had come. He sat and worked in a blind wretchedness, in a silence broken only by his own hammer tapping, or the rain, or sometimes only by the click of his stitching-needle. He sank into an even lower wretchedness at the thought of his father and the past. All his life had sprung from his father; he began to see it very clearly as the days went on. He could think of nothing of importance in all his life in which his father had not played a part, and when the rains ended and he could go back to the meadows and the river again he saw it more clearly still, the thought of a life without him half-frightening him like the expectation of a terror.

He went back to see his aunt at the beginning of December. She seemed half-angry at the long interval he had taken to think over her proposals. He did not tell her that he had scarcely thought of them at all.

'You haven't been up to the old games again?' she said.

'Ain't seen a rabbit for long enough,' he said.

She poured the wine with some of her old air of down-rightness, striking the cork of the bottle into place with a great blow of her hand.

'What made you come at all?' she said.

He was drinking his wine as she spoke and he wiped his lips on the back of his hand before speaking again.

'Seems Hester's goin' to have a baby,' he said.

She took up her own wine-glass without a trace of surprise. 'Who?' she asked.

'Reeves. Him as died. They told me to-day.'

'It doesn't surprise you, does it?'

'Wouldn't matter if it did. But if I go into the lawyer's, will you see the gal's all right?'

'She'll be all right.'

As though in silent thanks he took up his wine-glass and drank again, remembering as he did so how often they had sat there and bantered each other ironically. He felt curiously chastened now.

'Dad knowed,' he said.

For some reason she did not answer.

'Now I know what made him so bad about Reeves and Baron. I know now.'

Again she did not answer and he sat in thought, remembering Reeves and harvest-time and his father's anger.

It was his aunt who spoke at last.

'So you'll go into the lawyer's?' she said.

'Ah,' he said. He had scarcely given it a moment's conscious thought; he was only vaguely aware that he wanted to escape from the past he had known with his father, into a strange future in which the memory of him could have no place.

'It's either that, or 'list,' he said.

And for a moment he rather fancied himself as a soldier, until she burst upon him half-furiously:

'*I* should like!' she cried. '*I* should like!'

'Worse things,' he said. 'You can only get shot.'

'You can do that here!' she flashed.

It silenced him. He went back at once into the old apathy of acquiescence, listening to her proposals without protest, ready to exchange the blind wretchedness of his loss for anything.

'How would it be,' she said, 'if you came up, two or three nights a week, and bettered your handwriting a bit? Two nights handwriting, say, and one figures.'

'Ah, I'd better. I'm like a bull at haystack holding a pen.'

'And then, sometime after Christmas, you could start.'

She rose from her chair, picked up the wine and filled up his glass with an air of quiet solicitude.

'And when does that baby come?' she said.

'God a'mighty knows. Christmas, I shouldn't wonder.'

'How would it be, then, if you made a fresh start in the New Year?' she said.

He picked up his glass and then nodded in silence. He would make a new start, begin a new life. The old was finished.

PART TWO: THE MURDER

CHAPTER I

I

DURING the remaining days of December and on into the early days of January he went to the house as she had suggested, two or three evenings a week, or even more if the weather were bad, and she gave him lessons in handwriting and simple arithmetic. He would sit on one side of the table and she on the other, a pale rose tasselled shawl spread over the mahogany and a sheet of newspaper over the shawl to catch the ink-drops. They would begin with a glass of wine and end with one. It was so warm and comfortable there, with the fire and the wine, that a curious sense of pleasant lethargy would come over him, a feeling that nothing mattered. She set him exercises to copy, exercises of un-exacting simplicity which only heightened that sense of un-ambitious lethargy. And seeing him sometimes grow bored with the slow copying or multiplication she would suggest that he read instead. 'We'll both read,' she would say. 'What book shall it be, eh?' And he would say, 'Don't matter to me.' Then she would pick up the lamp and take it to the book-shelves and make a pretence of searching among the titles. 'Supposing we read Fox's *Martyrs*?' The book was always the same and as she read from it, slowly and smoothly, knowing the words off by heart, he would fall half-asleep in that dim atmosphere of wine and soft words and mellow lamp-light.

And gradually, from the lengthening of it all, the lethargy itself began to grow habitual. He was vaguely conscious of going physically soft. He no longer got up in the early morning; the days on which he had helped to towel Reeves in the first cold daylight seemed like the days of another life. In the mornings now he would lie in bed until he could hear his

71

mother's movements downstairs and the hiss of frying bacon, and he would come downstairs with a half-sleepy slouch, sitting huddled before the fire in his shirt-sleeves, unwashed, until she brought his breakfast. The days went past him like so many beads on a string, one like another. He slipped gradually and unconsciously into a state of physical degeneration. His muscles lost their tightness like a bladder slowly losing its air. And he did not notice the change in himself until, following one day with the hounds, his wind broke and the dead flabbiness of his muscles would not carry him, his legs weighing him down and his heart thundering against the pain of his lungs. After that, remembering his father and the length of their runs together and that steady, inexhaustible stride of Bishop's, he felt half-ashamed. Going to bed with a strong desire to reform himself and to renew the runs in the early morning, he woke early the next morning, remembered, and then got out of bed and went to the window. In the winter morning darkness it was raining bitterly, in a wild wind. And as he heard the wind tearing across the empty darkness of the river valley and everywhere the heavy running bitterness of the rain his enthusiasm vanished and he went back to bed.

He went on like this, resolving and doing nothing and sinking into an even lower lethargy and degeneration, not caring if he went into the lawyer's office or even what he did or what happened to him, until the day his sister's baby was born. The child was born in the early afternoon and he could hear his sister's intermittent cries all morning above the noise of his hammer in the tapping-shop. Towards noon he left the shop and went up into the house, calling upstairs when he found the rooms downstairs empty. No one answered him. He could hear only the dull grunting moans of Hester and the lowered voices of Sal and his mother. He called again and there was no answer. Then as he stood there his mother came downstairs, her gipsyish hair straggling down over her face and her sleeves rolled to the elbows. She went past him into the kitchen as though he did not exist and he followed her, half-complaining: 'Ain't there going to be no dinner?'

She came to life in a flash at his words. 'What dinner you have in this house to-day, you get yourself!'

Before he could answer she hurried past him upstairs and he stood there at a loss, half-mechanically rolling down his shirt-sleeves, half-stupidly listening to the renewed sound of moans and voices from above.

And suddenly, sick of it all and sick of himself, he took off his leather-stained shoe-apron and put on his jacket and his black muffler and cut himself some slices of bread and cheese in the kitchen, stuffing some of the bread into his mouth and then folding the cheese between the rest, as his father had always done, and putting it into his pocket.

Outside the air was cold, with a sense of snow. He walked quickly as he went through the town, skirting behind the Square, and out towards the bare flat country. As he walked across the wintry fields the wind came straight from the east into his face. He could see the clouds extending into the farthest distance like a series of shaggy waves, infinitely grey and sombre. He felt a sense of relief and pleasure as he walked and looked at the familiar country, deserted except for the sheep lying quiet under the hedges in the treeless fields and the flocks of peewits feeding on the dark ploughed land.

As he reached the higher country above Tichmarsh, under the shelter of the great belt of woods, the wind seemed to quieten down. He climbed the slope and looked back: the village with its square-towered church, the little white pub, the quiet bare fields beyond were all as familiar to him as his own hands. And for the first time in his life it gave him a conscious pleasure simply to stand there and look at it all.

It began to snow a little as he went on and down through the woods on the other side of the hill. The soft vague flakes seemed to be falling from the shaken branches of the trees. He hardly noticed them. Under the trees, out of the wind, there was a curious winter stillness over everything, the birds hushed, the rabbits rustling the dead leaves quietly.

Suddenly as he came out from under the trees into an open stretch of road it began to snow thickly and fiercely. The snow was driven out of the east in a great white cloud. He went on in spite of it, not sheltering, only turning up his jacket collar with the old habitual careless gesture of one hand. It was the first snow of the winter. It began to fall with increasing heaviness as he went on, as though it had been pent up somewhere, the large soft flakes already whitening the grass and the exposed branches of the higher trees. Then gradually the land became deserted. Nothing moved across it except himself and the endless flakes of snow. The feeling of the cold silence and the solitude and the snow itself refreshed him. The snowflakes covered his chest with a thick pad of white. His eyes were dazzled by the frenzy of falling flakes and the whiteness of the earth where the snow had settled.

At the foot of the slope it began to snow even faster and he turned and began to retrace his steps. The road was covered now, the snow like white velvet, his footsteps sound- less. Looking back he could see the blackish prints his soles had made in the road, and then, farther beyond the road and the trees, the infinite whitish darkness of the snow coming thickly out of the east, as though it would never end.

Back at the crest of the hill he left the road and struck away diagonally across the fields; almost mechanically, in spite of the snow he found the old path that he and his father had used. The grassland was already white, the grass crisp under the thickness of snow. As he went across the first pasture a rabbit limped away from him towards the lower hedge, its ears flat in fright against its neck. The rabbit moved awkwardly, in alternate runs and jumps, as though lame. And almost without thinking he began to run after it. The rabbit began to run a little faster as he hunted it, making for the hedge. Luke ran in half-stooping fashion, his hands low and outstretched, the speed of his running increasing the speed of the snow until he was half-blinded. Finally the rabbit disappeared; then as he reached the hedge he saw it again, skulking against the slope of the ditch. Before he could do anything it had begun to move again, running along the ditch with the same limping movement, and he followed it, running along the bank with the same outstretched attitude of his hands.

Suddenly, almost at the end of the ditch, he came to a standstill. He let the rabbit make its escape through the hedge-bottom into the field beyond. He stood in the ditch and stared.

A man was lying in a strange attitude, face upwards, in the ditch. The snow had ceased a little. A few flakes had fallen on the dead face without melting and on the fair stiff moustache.

Standing there, staring, wiping the half-wet flakes of snow from his face as though he could not see, Luke felt a rush of sickness and terror. He saw even before he bent down and moved the body a little and wiped a few of the snowflakes from the stiff face and then wiped his hands mechanically on his breeches that the man was the keeper, Baron. Having once moved he stood there as though frozen, not knowing what to do. His hands hung straight and limp against his flanks. A look of extreme terror rested on Baron's face. It seemed to communicate itself to him, doubling his own.

It began to snow heavily again as he stood there. Staring at the dead keeper, he was not conscious of the snow. The large light flakes began to fall on the keeper's face. They came down with great force. They were so thick and white that he could not see. And momentarily he suffered an hallucination. It seemed to him for a moment that the keeper was no longer there.

He began to walk away. After a yard or two he paused and looked back. He saw the keeper again with unexpected clarity. He could see now that there was blood on his chest. He could see it because the fresh snow had turned quite crimson in a small patch below the heart. The buttons of the jacket had been shattered; he could see the ragged threads of cotton hanging where the buttons had once been.

He began to move away again, half-running instinctively. Almost immediately he stopped again. A voice was shouting in the next field. It was a woman's voice; she seemed to be calling in her hens from the snow. Her voice was raised in a fine wail, the snow and the wind deadening it at intervals and snatching it away.

The next moment he saw her. She was coming up the field. Her apron, dirty white against the snow, was hooded over her head and she was clasping its corners close under her chin, wailing for the hens as she came along. 'Chucka! Chucka! Chuck! Chucka!' He stood alert, watching her. And then, lifting her head to let out a fresh wail and to search the field, she saw him.

Something in his alertness and terror arrested her immediately. He did what he knew to be a foolish thing almost before he had done it; the consciousness of his foolishness and the act itself were almost simultaneous. He ducked swiftly under the hedge. She saw him. And there was a second of silence before she let out a high wail of alarm. It was surprised from her almost involuntarily. The words were lost on him, smothered by the snow and driven away by the wind. But their tone of frantic alarm was so unmistakable that he went sick with fresh terror. He stood for another second as though frozen there. The woman's alarm rose into accusation. She was running up the field. He could hear her feet slithering wildly in the snow. 'I see ye! I see ye!' As she came nearer he caught for the first time the words she was shouting. It did not strike him until that moment that she was coupling him with her lost hens.

But by that time it was too late. He was already running wildly up the field.

2

Before the end of the afternoon he was already in strange country. It was still snowing. The snow was above the tops

76

of his boots. The road and the grass had been levelled into one unrippled surface from hedge to hedge, the drifts rising against the hedges in deep wind-smoothed arcs. The fields were empty of everything except that deep whiteness, the ploughed lands as white as the roads and the pastures.

He was walking steadily. His terror and the foolishness that had come with it had almost vanished. A little remained, enough to rise up at intervals and fill him with a brief sickness and panic again. He was walking now with a solitary purpose. He knew now that there was only one thing for him to do; he must go on in a wide circle, as his father had so often done, bearing to the eastward and then gradually to northward, and so back to Nenweald under cover of the snow and the darkness. He knew that he had already gone almost far enough to the east. The notion that he might be connected with the dead keeper had scarcely occurred to him. The memory of the dead face under the hedge, except for its horror, did not touch him. He was safe from it. It had nothing to do with him. Once his terror and horror had vanished he had only one fear, the fear of the woman's voice wailing its accusation at him across the field. His desire to escape from it was habitual, almost unconscious. It occurred to him once or twice that the woman was looking not for her hens, but for Baron himself. Even that did not alarm him, since his father had long since taught him never to meet trouble until it came.

When he turned from the road at last and began to bear to the east, meeting the wind, he began for the first time to feel tired. He had eaten nothing since morning. His eyes and limbs ached from the perpetual whiteness and heaviness of snow. Then with something like joy he remembered the bread and cheese in his pocket. He began to eat it as he walked along.

He had scarcely begun to eat the bread and cheese when he saw the shepherd's hovel. The straw hurdles had been built together under a high hedge of hawthorn, near the road. The wind and the snow, coming together, flung themselves against him furiously. Almost without pausing to think he climbed the field gate and went into the hovel, not seeing the shepherd there until he had sat heavily down on the straw.

The shepherd sat in the corner of the hut, half-covered with straw. He gazed at Luke with mild eyes, unastonished. Sitting down, Luke felt for the first time the completeness of his own exhaustion. When the shepherd spoke he answered mechanically. The bread and cheese thickened his words. The fragrance of dry straw and the calm in the hut after the wind were blissful. He discovered that he had hardly the strength to knock the snow off his chest.

'Come far?' said the shepherd.

'About far enough,' he said, 'in this.'

He had almost finished the bread and cheese before the shepherd spoke again. The sheep dog, a big shaggy iron-coloured dog, had come over to him to lick his hands. The warm moist caressing motion of the dog's tongue seemed to deepen his weariness.

'I don't recollect you,' the shepherd said. 'Where ye going?'

'Nenweald.' He said it without thinking and without surprise.

'Out o' your way, ain't ye?'

He did not answer the words and did not think much about them. The dog went on licking his hands, the motion soothing him. Outside it was snowing harder than ever. Stray flakes floated down into the hut, settling lightly on the straw. Looking at the snow he saw for the first time that the sky was growing visibly darker. 'What clock is it?' he said. This time the shepherd did not answer. He was looking at the blood that had dried on the fingers of Luke's right hand. The dog's wet mouth had heightened the colour of it from sepia to pink. Luke looked at it too. Until that moment he had not seen it. He had not even suspected that he might have blood on his hands. Half-mechanically he picked up

78

some of the snow that had fallen from his chest and began to wash off the blood. Then he remembered as he did so why he had not seen it before. He had walked all the time with his hands in his pockets. The spasm of fear that had shot up in him at the sight of the blood vanished immediately.

Without thinking, he got up to go. While he was standing at the door of the hut, watching the snow falling still as thick as ever but now out of an increasingly darker sky, the dog ran out into the field. Turning, he saw that the shepherd had risen too.

'We may as well go together,' he said.

They walked out of the hut and across the field and into the road. The snow was half up to their knees and the dog buried to its shoulders. After the shelter of the hedge and the calmness in the hut the wind seemed furious. The shepherd walked slowly. Luke, tired, fell into the same pace, a sudden feeling of irresolution coming over him, a feeling that he did not want to go on.

He began to feel also, as they walked slowly on against the wind, that he would not get back to Nenweald that night. At first the thought was scarcely conscious. It was a mere sensation, a vague part of his physical weariness. It was only when something made him ask the shepherd 'How far would Nenweald be from here?' and he heard the shepherd answer, 'Thirteen or fourteen miles,' that the thought leapt into full consciousness. He could hardly realize even then, in spite of his weariness, how far he had come. He knew vaguely that it was the dead heaviness and the stark whiteness of the snow that had made him so tired. The distance was nothing. Looking back, he could retrace every step of it. It was only when he looked forward, into the infinite distance of darkness and snow, that he began to feel desperate and afraid.

He began to see also how foolish he had been. He ought never to have run from the woman's accusing voice. He saw that now. What had made him run? Why had he done that? He began to see the folly of it so clearly that his fear returned.

79

It came back to him in a spasm of anguish and shivering, the shivering so physical and evident that the shepherd saw it.

'You ain't very hot, I know.'

He made a supreme effort to speak. The words did not come and he felt a spasm of anger against himself. He heard the shepherd say:

'You better come along o' me and git thawed a bit.'

'No, I'll git along,' he said.

He was talking mechanically, with some unconscious part of himself. He did not want to refuse. He did not want to go on.

'The missus'll be glad to give you some tea.'

'No,' he said again, 'I'll git along.'

Even as he spoke he was amazed at the depth of his own folly and obstinacy. He tried to struggle with it. It was then that he discovered how weak he was. He could scarcely lift his feet through the weight of snow. His hands were numb. His folly arose out of pure weakness, out of a kind of strengthless perversity. He knew even before the shepherd spoke again that he could not go on.

They walked along the road for almost another mile before the shepherd spoke. It was still snowing. The wind seemed to be blowing the darkness across the endlessly flat fields from the east, a darkness of snow and twilight together.

'The missus'll git on to me,' the shepherd said, 'if I tell her and you don't come in.'

They came to a solitary yellow brick house that stood in the roadside behind a thicket of holly trees. From a lamp shining in one of the windows the light fell yellow on the snow. There was no other house in sight. The land stretched out into the same infinite flatness on all sides, as though the snow had levelled it. Looking at that desolate flatness of strange country he had no need to think before he spoke again.

'All right,' he said. 'I'll come in.'

As they left the road and walked towards the house he felt the loneliness of the place. It gave him a sense of security.

3

When he came out of the house again darkness had fallen, but the snow had ceased. The shepherd came as far as the road with him, shining a lantern, advising him: 'Be a good tip if you went back past the hovel, that way, the way you come.' He began to go back along the road, the shepherd waving the lantern. He turned up the collar of his jacket as he walked, holding it together under his chin with one hand, grasping the ash-stick the shepherd had given him in the other. The stick had been whittled at the knob into the shape of a dog's head and worn to the smoothness of ice by prolonged use. The smooth feeling of the stick, the presence of the shepherd and the light of the lantern on the snow gave him a feeling of immense assurance. When at last he turned round again the shepherd had gone and he could not see the house in the darkness.

He began to walk with the old steadiness. The wind had died down with the snow, but now it was freezing bitterly. The air was quiet and more brittle at every step he took. He was no longer tired. The snow, dried and lightened already by the fierceness of frost, was very soft and almost pleasant to walk upon. It scarcely checked his progress.

As he walked he made his calculations, how he would walk steadily on in the snow, and how, reckoning it then to be five o'clock and reckoning the shepherd's distance to Nenweald correct, he would be home before nine o'clock. He let his mind run on in expectation. He had already made his decision as to the way he would go. He would go straight back, keeping to the roads and the villages, calling perhaps at the White Hart for a pint and a rest. He would hear something there of the murder. Then he began to see what had never occurred to him in his panic and folly, that it might not have been a murder at all, but simply a suicide, even an accident. In the clear frost-quiet air, after the warmth and the rest of the shepherd's house, he felt extraordinarily rational. All his fears except one had vanished. That was the fear of the woman's wailing at him across the field. And he was troubled less and less even by that as he went on.

The sky began to clear and a star or two came out, shining as though with frost, as he walked. The snow had covered the tracks he had made in the early afternoon. It was light enough, with the few stars and the strange light coming up from the snow, for him to see that.

He found the roads easily, though he was tiring again by the time he reached the crest of the hill above Tichmarsh. He could feel the familiarity of the country then, recognizing the woods and the trees as he came to them. Some of his fear returned as he climbed the slope, trickling back thinly like the cold in his veins and his weariness.

It came back in an overpowering and sudden rush as he began to go down the slope by the field where he had run away from the woman in the afternoon. It came back with such force that he came to an abrupt standstill. His heart was like ice. His hands fell from the sheer weight of their own weakness against his legs.

Half-way down the hill the road was blocked with a crowd of people. He could hear the confused whisper of their voices. The darkness was filled with excitement. He could see the black shape of a trap drawn up across the road, the light yellow on the wheels and the road. He could hear the dull thudding of restless and stamping feet in the snow. The sound made a soft thunder of accompaniment to the inarticulate whisper of voices rising and falling in the still air.

He stood there for a minute in a kind of strengthless immobility. He was breathing very fast, in a series of irregular gasps, through his mouth. It was his only physical motion. The rest of him seemed to have become lifeless, just as his mind had become dead except for a single repeated thought.

'I'm done for,' he kept thinking. 'I'm done for.'

He acted at last from an impulse of pure terror. The

impulse that had made him run from the woman in the field made him move again. He was still a hundred yards or more from the lights. He went across the verge of the road with a suddenness of activity which startled even himself, moving with extreme softness in the snow. Then once over the fence in the field, he began to run. He ran doubled up, keeping to the hedge, where the snow was thinnest, running almost the length of the field before breaking through the hedge and traversing the corner of the field beyond.

It was only then that he realized where he was. The field was the one from which the woman and her wailing voice had hounded him in the afternoon. He turned at once and broke back through the hedge, running westwards, falling and slithering across the ditches in the haste and panic of his fresh terror.

He ran on like that, scrambling and falling up to his waist in the drifts and the ditches, until he could no longer see the lanterns or hear the voices.

4

Though he had only a vague idea of it then and did not know it for certainty until long after, the roads to the east and south of Nenweald were blocked that night at all points of importance by little squads of police and volunteers. They were searching, in spite of the warning the woman had given in the afternoon, not for him, but for a young soldier, a deserter. He knew that, too, only long afterwards. As he ran and slithered on in the darkness and the snow, he was never without the conviction that they were searching for him. The thought renewed alternately his strength and terror. He kept as much as he could to the fields, running under the protection of the hedges. Occasionally he went through a belt of woodland. There, under the trees, where the snow had scarcely covered the leaves, it was easier for him. The whole countryside was silent. There seemed to be no life, nothing moving about the snow except himself, and the quietness

83

seemed ominous. It froze bitterly as he went on, a still, black frost. The stars increased, flashing as though frozen also. He left the Pole star on his right hand, and a little behind him, conscious of a feeling of greater safety when his face was turned to the south.

As he went on he gave up, unconsciously, the thought of returning home. It already seemed years since he had left it. He wanted only to escape and if possible to rest. When he did rest it was only for brief intervals. He sprawled against a fence or squatted under a hedge, panting and choking with great gasps for breath. He felt that if he ever sat down he would never get up again. So he rested as little as possible. He would go to what he thought was the limit of his physical endurance, and then beyond it, and then to what he thought was the limit again, and then beyond that, saying to himself: 'I'll get through another field, I'll get past the end of the hedge, I'll get through another field,' the words repeated and repeated in time with the heavy running sound of his feet. Finally, resting in a wood, half-kneeling, still not daring to sit down, he was so utterly exhausted that, as he knelt there on the snowless leaves of oak and hazel, he rubbed his hands to and fro across his face for the sheer comfort of his own touch. And doing so, he caught the smell of leather on his hands, the still strong greasy odour of the boots he had been making that morning. It gave him an inexplicable sense of comfort. And as he sat there he ran his hands over his face again and again, smelling the leather smell eagerly until finally he felt that it had given him back his strength.

Soon after he had gone on again he came to a road; he was standing on it before he was aware of it. And stopping to consider where he was and which way he should take, he felt for the first time the desperation and hopelessness of his everlasting misery. He saw clearly how things had worked and were working against him: the woman's cry of accusation, the blood the shepherd had seen on his hands, his own foolishness. Then he began to see that they were all little or nothing against the fact that he was a poacher, that his father had been a poacher, and that his father had hated Baron and had gone about the countryside threatening revenge. Lastly he saw that he himself might be suspected of revenge too. If the police were looking for anybody at all they were looking for him. And curiously, through all the years of poaching and defiance of the law, he had never been in the hands of the police. It was the thing he dreaded above all others.

And standing there, trying to make up his mind which way to go and with the thought of his father and the police and his own folly and hopelessness coming back to him, he heard the sound of feet in the snow.

For some reason he could not run. The footsteps were coming rapidly towards him. But he stood as though frozen, waiting for them to come. He was almost resolved at that moment to surrender.

He had no sooner thought of it than he wanted to run. And almost simultaneously he knew that it was too late. Whoever it was coming along the road had seen him. They were calling him. There were two voices. For some reason they did not alarm him. He listened to them quite calmly. Finally he went towards them with almost a sense of relief.

It was not until he saw the figures of the two constables and they began questioning him that his fear returned. It shot up in him in a single spasm and died. After that he could only stand there and listen and answer their questions in a kind of resigned stupor.

'Who are you? What are you doing? Where are you going?' Their questions seemed part of some mechanical rigmarole learnt off by heart. He answered mechanically too, his answers coming to his astonishment smoothly, meekly, without effort.

'I'm looking for a dog.'

'What dog? What sort of dog?'

'Black. He's only a pup.'

'What's your name?'

'Simpson.'

'What are you doing along this road?'

'I'm looking for the dog. I told you.'

'This road don't go nowhere.'

'The dog don't know that.'

His old drawling tone of contempt astounded him.

'None o' your chelp. We've got serious business on. What did you say your name was?'

'Simpson.'

'Remember that, Joe.'

'Fred Simpson.'

'Fred Simpson. Remember that.'

He stood there apathetic and half-indifferent, not knowing how he made up the lies and sustained them, not caring whether they were believed or not. Finally one of the constables began to repeat the name he had given, speaking in a tone half-ruminative, half-ominous. 'Simpson, Simpson. It seems familiar. Simpson?' and at last:

'Where'd you say you came from?'

'Nowhere particular.'

Without warning the constable reached out and snatched off his hat, leaning nearer as he did so to look at his black hair and sallow face.

'I thought so. A gyppo.'

Then, just as he had done in the field when the woman had seen him first, he did a thing he knew to be foolish even before he had done it. He lifted his fist and struck the constable powerfully in the mouth, knocking him backwards in the snow. He felt the sharp pain of the man's teeth on his knuckles as though the mouth had been opened in protest or astonishment. It was a brief sharp pain, exhilarating. By the time it had vanished he was running up the road, the second constable after him, shouting.

He ran madly. Half-turning to look back after a moment or two he saw that the constable had given up, had gone back to help the other. It made no difference to him. He continued to run.

It was only when he was in the fields again, still running

and slithering desperately along the ditches, that he remembered his cap. The constable still had it. He remembered a second later that he had also lost the stick the shepherd had given him. The stick and the cap: clues against him. And as he went on his thoughts seemed to become concentrated into a single repeated phrase of despondency and despair: 'You're done for now, you're done for, you're done for.'

CHAPTER II

I

HE came out of the church soon after seven o'clock in the morning. It was still dark. The snow had frozen everywhere into a bitter ice. It was as smooth as glass in the footprints and cart-ruts along the road. The church was under repair. Scaffold planks were half-buried by snow under the shelter of the walls outside, the nave cluttered with the straw tool bags of the workmen and the still unsawn planks against which he had knocked his shins as he blundered about in the darkness of the night before.

The church stood solitary, apart from its village, and the road went downhill away from it. He walked rapidly. In the east the black winter morning darkness was just touched with light. As the thin colourless break in the blackness widened he began to see the road, then the hedges, then the expanse of fields and woods under the snow. He was walking along the top of a ridge. There were many woods: young spruce spinneys and thin old woods of oak or pine. The pines held the snow in great cakes on their thick needles. As the light came up he looked for a landmark. But he could see nothing, not even a spire, that was familiar. It was strange country. It looked even stranger and more remote under the snow. Once, turning, he looked back for the church. It had vanished, cut off by the thick woodland. He went on with a feeling of increasing loneliness. He felt strangely cut off from the world, from his own fears and also from the events of the day before. The stillness of the air was bitter. There was no hope of warmth; the sun came up slowly, whitish and cold. Then he ran a little way in the first cold sunlight, pumping his arms and stamping his feet. He had taken off his boots in the church in order to rest and dry his feet, and in the stone coldness his feet had got still colder and the circulation had never begun again. After a few yards he gave up the running. For some reason his body seemed empty of strength and the frozen air, breathed fast, as like a series of bitter stabs at his lungs.

He stood still at last to rest. And standing there, thinking that what was the matter with him was not the cold or the weariness, but only that he had not eaten anything, he saw for the first time the river flowing in the low-lying land under the ridge. It was a wide stream, intricate and slow-flowing. Vanishing and reappearing among the copses on its banks it went away finally into a distance of level meadows. The water was sluggish and drab with snow, a yellowish colour. He stood arrested, startled for the moment into the wild thought that it was the river he had known all his life. Then he saw that he did not know it at all. He could see, even under the thickness of the snow, that there was no towing path. The meadows came flat and unchecked to the water's edge. Not that it mattered. He went on again. The road turned with a bend in the ridge, and the river, cut off for a moment by a copse of fir, reappeared. He saw it flowing away into the flat country illimitably white with snow. Not that it mattered. Not that anything mattered. If he was done for, he was done for. He had gone beyond the extent of his own fears into a listlessness of indifference. He only wanted to eat.

Once the thought of eating had entered his mind he could not shift it. His hunger and the cold were part of one another. His thoughts of eating became part of them both, persistent and increasing. Thinking of the food he forgot the constables, the woman crying after him up the field, the shepherd, the dead face of the keeper under the hedge. They merged together into a meaningless past. He even forgot what they had ever meant to him.

He went on for almost another mile before the consciousness of what he was doing struck him fully. He was looking for houses, now, where he had previously wanted to avoid them. The realization of it came to him without fear, without an emotion of any kind at all. It was a fact. He had not the strength to dispute the wisdom or the folly of it any longer.

He had gone beyond the river, and out of sight of it, when he came to the first house. He stood by the hedge, on the roadside. He stood up to his knees in drift that had piled up under the hedge. He looked at the place. It was a small farmhouse: there was a hen-yard between the hedge and the front porch, and beyond, in the fenced-in paddock, a bush-hovel housing a trap and a land-cart and odds and ends of litter and harness. He could see it all clearly in the rising light, against the white background of snow. He stood staring. He stood for perhaps five minutes, taking in the place, making up his mind. During that time he saw no signs of life. The snow across the hen-yard was clean and level, just as it had fallen. He could see where the wind had driven the snow in a smooth arc against the front door, which had not been opened.

He waited a little longer. Then he went round to the back of the house. The view was almost the same: the untrodden hen-yard, the smooth snowdrift against the unopened door. But now he could see the hens, in a low wired-in coop half-covered by sacks that the wind and snow had frozen against the wire. The coop stood four or five yards from the hay-stack behind which he was standing. He could see the hens, about a dozen of them, reddish-brown and white, huddled together on the muck-caked perches.

He was standing there looking at them, wondering at the silence of the place, when the back door opened. A woman came out. She came straight across the yard, in a direct line for him, rapidly, as though she had seen him. He took a single look at her and then hid himself again, pressing himself flat against the stack.

He knew in another moment that it was all right, that she had come only to feed the hens. Nevertheless he dared not move. He stood rigid, hearing the great plods of her feet in the snow, the trap-door of the hen-house jerked up, her 'Tchk! Tchk!' to the hens. She seemed so near once, and her breath indrawn in such sharp gasps that he expected any moment to see her come behind the stack. And when nothing happened and he heard her return across the yard and shut the door, and he could hear nothing but the subdued flutter of the hens and their hard beak-taps on the food-bowl, he still could not move.

He stood for about a minute before daring to stir again. It seemed longer. He had pressed himself so hard against the stack that he was stiff. Looking out at last, he saw what the woman had brought the hens: two shallow bowls of bread-mash sprinkled and half-mixed with wheat bran. The mash was hot. He saw the vapour rising thinly from the bowls in the dark hen-house. Then he caught a breath of soft bran-smell and the steamy odour of hot sopped bread.

It smelled so warm and fragrant that he did not think before he acted. He took only a single look at the trapdoor in the hen-house. It was low down, about a foot from the floor. The string which held it went up over a little white china pulley and was tied to a hook in the woodwork. The bowls of hen food had been put on the floor, at arm's length from the trap. The hens had already half eaten them. Their rapid beak-taps, hard in the glazed stone bowls, were the only sounds in the frozen air.

He came out from behind the stack with amazing quietness and rapidity to pull up the trap-door. The string slipped with almost startling smoothness through his fingers, without a sound. Half-kneeling in the snow he did not trouble to look round to see if the woman were returning. He saw nothing but the bowls of mash and the pecking hens which he struck aside with his hands. He could reach the food-bowl easily. It was the hens which troubled him. He had scarcely put his hands through the trap-door when they set up their frightened squawking, making short flights of protest, falling over one another, clucking madly.

But the hens and the sounds they made did not trouble him for more than a second or two. He dragged the food-bowl desperately along the muck-caked floor of the hen-house, spilling the mash. Then he lifted it rapidly out through the trap-door. He began to eat almost before the trap-door had fallen again, scooping up the now warm mash with his hands, cramming it into his mouth, bolting it down, scarcely tasting it or knowing what he did.

He had already decided, half-consciously, to reach for the second bowl after he had eaten the first. And he was having a kind of race with the hens, feverishly looking at them from the corners of his eyes, when he heard the back door of the house open and the quick running plods of the woman's feet coming across the snow. Even then he did not look up. There was a little of the sop left in the bowl, the bottoms, more water than bread. He wanted to finish it. He would still have time to finish it and then run. The woman, with her large, heavy plodding feet, could never catch him.

It was only when she shouted at him 'Here!' and he looked up that he saw that it was too late to run. She was not more than four or five yards away when she shouted. He stood up-right, dropping the bowl simultaneously, cramming the wet sop into his mouth. Even then he felt that he could escape. He even began to run, looking first this way and then that, before she shouted again:

'Here, here! I want you! Here! I want you!'

All the strength and desire to run went out of him at once. He stood perfectly still. Only his mouth moved as he sucked down the last mouthful of mash. And as she came across the snow, moving with astonishing rapidity for so large a woman, he felt his body go listless.

She stood before him, panting. Her large bust swelled

91

under her tight cotton pinafore. It seemed almost a minute before she could speak.

'Burn you! What d'ye think I'm made on, eh? What made you take that hens' food?'

He did not answer. She had a rich, peremptory voice. It was full not so much of anger as astonishment.

'What made you?' she repeated.

He was silent.

'Why didn't you ask?'

He still said nothing. She, too, stood as though at a loss for fresh words. They stood like that for half a minute, his mind vacant, she still panting for breath.

It was she who spoke at last.

'Ain't I seen you somewhere?'

He stared, shaking his head wildly. Christ, he was done for.

'I know I seen you—somewhere. I don't know where, but somewhere.'

'No, no,' he said.

'Where d'ye come from?'

He did not answer. And she stood scrutinizing him as though to find some answer herself.

'Coming and nicking folks' hen-food, coming in here like that. Why didn't you ask?'

'I—'

'I know I'd seen you somewhere.'

'You're wrong, missus, you're—'

She cut him short again, the words like a thunderbolt:

'Ain't your name Bishop? Ain't that it?'

He went sick. 'No,' he said. 'No, no.' His voice was strained and a little wild. He had no control over it. 'No, no,' he kept saying. 'You're wrong, missus, you're wrong.'

She spoke again with a voice of unexpected quietness, almost as though to soothe him and set him at rest.

'I know your Dad,' she said. 'You can't get away from it. I know your Dad.'

'That's where you're wrong!' he said desperately. 'I ain't got one.'

'Not Buck Bishop? Ain't that him?'

'No,' he kept saying. 'No, No.'

And after a moment or two she seemed to give it up. She seemed to become for the first time conscious of his aspect of weariness and wild dejection. She stood looking searchingly at him: at the snow scattered and caked on his legs and chest, the thorn-scratches livid and half-dried on his face and hands, the strengthless droop of his arms at his side.

'You look gay,' she said.

'I feel it.'

He uttered the words almost defiantly. The next moment he regretted them. And as though in sudden contrition he said:

'That's right about me. What you said. It's right.'

'Why'd you say that about your Dad?'

'He's dead. That's why.'

She stood silent. Some of the hen-mash, now cold, still clung to his chin and mouth. She stood watching him lick it off, weakly. She could see that he was famished. His face was dead-white, the snow reflection driving away the last of its yellowish pallor.

'What are you doing out here?' she said at last. 'Where are you going?'

'Nowhere.'

'Ain't you got summat better to do than steal folks' hen-mash?'

He did not answer. And she said:

'Your Dad never learnt you fool's tricks like that, I warrant.'

Something in her words took the last of his resistance away from him. It was as though a trap-door opened inside him and all his fortitude and ease and even his physical control dropped suddenly through it beyond recovery. Tears began to run down his cheeks without warning, from sheer weakness, before he was aware of it. He

93

let them come without a motion or sign of resistance. As they rolled down his cheeks and into his half-opened mouth he had not the strength to utter a sound.

'You'd better come inside,' she said. 'Come on, come on.'

He followed her half-blindly across the yard.

2

Indoors, in the kitchen that looked out on the yard and the hen-house, he discovered how cold he was. Sitting over the fire, shuddering, he was so cold that he was not quite conscious of what was happening. She brought him a mug of coffee, with a bitter taste, like that of burnt parsnips. He drank it without knowing what it was. He expected every moment to hear other footsteps and other voices, but nothing happened. And after bringing him a hunch of bread and bacon and a second mug of coffee she came and sat by the the fire also. He felt sick, then, whenever he thought of the hen-mash. He put his hand over his mouth whenever he retched. His skin was like stone; he could feel the veins on the backs of his hands standing out like stiff hard tubes, as though the blood in them had frozen solid.

'You been out all night, I know,' she said at last. 'Ain't you?'

'Ah.' He had not the strength or control over himself to explain about the church. His face was so drawn and stiff that he hardly formed even the single syllable.

'You ain't done that for nothing,' she said.

He sat dumb and stupefied.

'What was it?' she said.

He tried to say something, but without success. His mouth opened and closed weakly.

'I knowed your Dad,' she said then. 'It's all right. I ain't going to give you away.'

'I—' He could go no further.

'Donkey's years,' she said. 'You're the spit on him. I bet

you ain't ever heard him talk o' Luce Strickland, but he knowed me all right.'

He spoke at last, forcing himself.

'I heard him talk o' Sam Strickland. Militiaman.'

'That's him. That's my chap.'

'One arm. I heard Dad talk o' that a lot.'

'That's it.'

He had nothing to say, and she went on:

'Your Dad used to come up here, fishing and I don't know what. Twenty or thirty years ago. I known him doss up at my chap's old home, time th'old mother was alive. Used to bring in old fiddle and sing-song, great times. Ye Dad had a rare voice. Yes, I knowed him. Knowed him well. Old Buck.'

As she was speaking he looked up, thinking he heard a sound in the snow outside, and she said:

'You needn't git worried. We don't see a soul up here, one week's end to another. Sam's gone into market, and he won't be back yit awhile.'

She ceased speaking suddenly. His face had gone a shade whiter than she had dreamed it possible. The skin of his lips was indistinguishable now from the rest of his face. As the faintness overtook him his eyes stiffened immovably, wide open, transfixing her, a frozen blue colour, the whites distended. She heard him groan. Before she could move or speak his body slipped forward and out of the chair as though down a plank of ice.

3

He did not realize how long he lay ill. After she had carried him upstairs that morning, unaided, lifting him bodily with astonishing strength, kicking open the half-latched door as she went, he did not remember much at all. He lay shuddering and sweating under the blankets. The hours and then the days went past him without troubling him. He sank down into a pit of utter weakness. And lying there, staring up at the far-off ceiling, very white at first with

95

the reflection of the snow, then darker as he grew weaker and the snow thawed in the hen-yard outside, he was concerned persistently for one thing. He wanted his cap, the cap the constable had snatched from him. He felt that his life depended on the cap. He reached at last a point of agony and desperation in which he saw with a kind of visionary sight the cap suspended from a hook in the ceiling. He yelled out for it. It was a yell of delirium and agony. It was followed by shouts, 'The cap, the cap! My cap!' He kept up the shouting at intervals for the rest of the day and into the night and then for part of the following day. On Strickland and his wife the effect was bewildering. The shout seemed meaningless. It could have no meaning beyond the meaning that it was a sign of delirium. At times, when the desire for the cap and the delirium at never getting it rose to a frenzy, Strickland would kneel on the bed and pin down Luke's arms, flat, like a wrestler. It subdued his body, but not the wild stare at the ceiling or the shout. It was only when the shout changed at last to 'The hook, the hook! It's on the hook!' that Strickland saw that it had any meaning at all. He went downstairs, then, and came back with a cap of his own. He was a tall lanky man and something occurred to him as he came back upstairs with the cap. Back in the bedroom he stood over the bed, upright, with the cap hanging on the iron hook of his wooden arm. He began to lower it gently. In a moment Luke saw it. On the bed Mrs. Strickland, pinning down with her own muscular hands his thin, nervous, incredibly agitated arms, felt the strength and the panic go suddenly out of them. They relaxed and fluttered and loosened and then fluttered again with a kind of nervous sigh. Gradually Strickland lowered the hook and the cap. Then Mrs. Strickland stood away from the bed. Then at last Luke half-raised himself in bed and took the cap in his hands.

He began gradually, from that moment, to improve. At the end of the week, three weeks after she had caught him with the bowl of hen-mash in his hands, Mrs. Strickland helped him to dress. He went downstairs and sat in the kitchen and stared at the fire. Nothing else interested him. The next day he put on his trousers himself, lacking the strength to do up more than half the buttons, and went downstairs again. He felt extraordinarily weak, but he stood for a long time looking out of the window. It was February. He could not believe that the snow had gone. He had a vague notion that he had been in the bedroom for a day or two, perhaps for three or four days, no more. He stood looking out of the window until he was too weak to stand any longer. Beyond the hen-yard and the paddock with its cart-hovel he could see a copse of birch and oak bordering a piece of wheatland. In the field the corn had come up thickly, in fine tangled threads of tender green, the rows curving with the land. He kept looking from the wheat to the birches. The trees were the colour of wine, a dark red, the buds and catkins shining more brightly here and there against the buds of oak, which were paler, a sand colour, showing up in turn against their darker branches. It was afternoon, the sky was cloudy, with intermittent breaks of sunshine. Then he began to see by the angle of the cold yellow light how long he must have been there and how near it was to spring.

At the end of the next week he could walk across the hen-yard. On fine afternoons he put on the cap which Strickland had held on his iron hook and which he had never asked him to return, and he would go into the yard with the corn-bowl to feed the hens. A few snowdrops, like big white violet buds, had come out by the house-wall. The sun was quite warm. The hens came running in from the paddock, long-legged, fluttering, to feed on the sun-brown corn he scattered down on the yard. He was still so weak that it was all he could do to hold the iron corn-bowls, and he would sit down sometimes on a box by the house-wall to rest. The sun was wonderful. After he had fed the hens he would still sit there, resting, spreading out his hands, feeling the sun softly soaking down into the weak veins. Then he would run his fingers through the handful of wheat and maize grains left in the bowl, feeling the sun on them also and on the iron.

He began to feel that it was time he was gone. He knew from Strickland, who was an old soldier and therefore interested in the case, that the young soldier had been captured. But he shrank from going. And though he knew he had nothing to fear he was still afraid. The old fear would rise up in him at times like a pain.

'I'd better be getting back,' he said at the end of another week.

'You ain't fit,' Strickland said.

'I seed ye s'afternoon,' Mrs. Strickland said, 'sitting on that box. Whacked wi' just feedin' a few hens. Y'ain't worth a hatful o' crabs. You stop here a bit, another week, and then see. We knowed your Dad. You're welcome.'

'Ain't much profit in it for you,' he said.

'Never you mind about profit.'

He had not the strength to resist their arguments or refuse. He stayed on another week. It was almost the end of February. The sun was very warm sometimes in the early afternoons, and he would sit under the cart-hovel, in the sun, and watch Strickland bush-harrowing the little paddock, patterning the grass in broad strips of light and shade. The thrushes would sing on, wonderfully, into the evenings. The evening light was clear and cold, the western sky over the woods a primrose green with frost. By the house the snowdrops had multiplied and soon the first crocuses were unfolding, bright yellow. And he began to see, gradually, that he did not want to go back. He would sit and reason quietly about it, contrasting the open fields and the cold spring solitude and the sunshine with the old life; the strange new country with the raw river-valley. He was beginning to see for the first time in his life that there was another way of living than the way he had always done.

He was still weak, but he was strong enough, now, to give Strickland a hand with the root-chopping and the swill-mixing and the grooming down of the horse, and he began to get back some of the confidence he had lost in himself. He worked quietly and slowly, his strength short. The farm was small, two arable fields and the paddock, and in the evenings he would round it, skirting the boundaries. At first he could do only half the distance. But gradually he did more than half, then the whole distance, going as far as the birch-copse he had seen from the windows. On the edge of the copse, by the brook that entered Strickland's land, the buds of primroses were already pale green. He could smell spring in the wood, in the water and in the drying earth of the corn-land.

One evening, as he came by the copse, a young rabbit broke from the cover of the dead winter-grass by the brook-side and tore across his path. He flung himself down, instantly, without thought, to catch it. As he fell flat the rabbit bounded away across the young corn and disappeared.

He lay there for some minutes without being able to move. The earth seemed to have struck him with stupendous force. He lay half-stunned, not able to realize it. When he stood up again he was trembling. He walked slowly back to the house. He felt shaken, broken up. He put his hands in his pockets at last and clenched them to stop their trembling.

The next day he could not go out. He had begun to let his moustache grow, and he sat rubbing his fingers gently backwards and forwards across the stiff short hairs, the slow repetitive movement soothing him a little. It was all he could do to keep from crying at the return of his weakness. There was no pain. It was as if his body were empty, as if the fall against earth had knocked away all the fortitude and strength he had got back again.

The Stricklands were worried at his inactivity; and that evening Strickland said:

'If you want to go back I'll git the trap out and drive you over to-morrow.'

'How far is it?' he said. 'I could very like walk that step or two.'

'You'd look well, walking.'

'How far is it?'

'How far is it, missus? Would it be sixteen?'

'Be a good sixteen. Very like seventeen,' she said.

'Knowed the time,' said Strickland, 'when your Dad'd walk that and back in a day. But you ain't him.'

'All right,' he said. 'You drive me back.'

He felt a curious feeling of despondency at the thought of departure. He had not realized he had come so far. They were to start on the following morning, when Strickland had fed the stock, but when morning came he knew that he did not care whether they started at all.

'Which way d'ye reckon going?' he said.

'I reckoned Souldrop way,' said Strickland.

'Ain't there no other way? All my mother's kin spring from there.'

'That's the way I reckoned.'

Luke stood for a moment, thinking.

'I ain't going,' he said. 'I don't want to go.'

'You please yourself. But we're only poor folks and we can't—'

'I'll work,' he said. 'I want to work.'

'I'd give you work if I could,' said Strickland. 'But I ain't in a big way. I can't do it.'

'Getting up at five and working till dark—you could do with a hand.'

'I know, but I can't do it.'

'Ain't there nobody else?'

'You ain't fit,' said Strickland. 'You ain't fit to work.'

'I want to work,' he said. 'I want to work. Ain't there nobody?'

He stood there in earnest desperation, his whole body wrought up against its own weakness, until Strickland said at last:

'There's Thompson, Elijah Thompson. You couldn't do no less'n ask.'

'What kind o' man is he?'

'Elijah? Methodist man. Local preacher.'

'Where's his place?'

They walked across the hen-yard to the gate by the road

and Strickland pointed out the way to the farm across the fields.

'You'll see it. Big stone place. Damson orchard. You can't miss it.'

Luke crossed the road and began to walk slowly away across the fields. The footpath, raised up, went along by a low hedgeside above a ditch. An east wind was blowing and now and then the wind caught him, making him stagger, and in concern Strickland stood watching him stagger along until he had gone from sight.

CHAPTER III

I

ELIJAH THOMPSON had gone that morning to buy heifers at a neighbouring farm, and the kitchen-girl told Luke to come back again in the early evening. When he walked across the fields again in the cold clear twilight the wind was dropping, but the furrows in the ploughed lands were bleached white on the eastern side, and in the cornfields the young flourishing shoots of winter wheat lay flattened against the earth by the cold wind as though by a roller. All about the big stone farmhouse the damson trees, very old and uncoloured yet by blossom-buds, stood out black against the wind-cleared sky. When he arrived at the farm the hands had knocked off, the hens were cooped up for the night, and there was a strange evening silence everywhere. Then when the kitchen-girl opened the door to him she put her hand up to her mouth in half-frightened fashion. The family were at evening prayers.

He stood in the half-dark passage running from the kitchen door to the parlour and waited for them to finish. The young girl, nervous and silent, waited at his side. They stood together without exchanging a word until the last words of the last prayer had been spoken. He could hear at first two thin uncertainly upraised soprano voices joined together by the sombre harmony of Thompson's bass, then the solitary voice of Thompson reading the scripture, and finally the repetition of the benedictory prayer. It reminded him of his mother and his childhood. When the sounds ceased at last the girl knocked at the door. Thompson asked for it to be opened. The girl, as though scared by the voice, gave the wooden knob a single jerk, and scurried back along the passage, leaving him there alone, slightly apprehensive and not knowing what to do, until Thompson called out:

'Well, well, whoever it is, come in, come in.'

He went into the room with his cap in his hands.

'Well?' Thompson said. 'Well?'

Like his wife and daughter, Thompson was still standing, as he must have been doing during the prayers, with the Bible still in his hands, his forefinger still marking the page. He was a large man, with a receding scalp crowned with abundant dark red, almost calf-coloured hair, very stiff, and large ears in the hollows of which the hair grew thickly also. He was wearing spectacles, but he wrenched them off as Luke entered. He folded them up flat and then without thinking substituted them for his finger as the book-mark, taking them out again a moment later with a gesture of impatience, as though remembering it were some profanity.

'I don't know you,' he said.

'I come up from Strickland's place, looking for work.'

'Work?'

Thompson laid the Bible on the table. The Bible was a black octavo, but he held it in one of his exceedingly large red-haired hands almost as lightly as though it were a young bird.

'What work? What kind of work?'

'Anything.'

'Anything?'

Thompson looked at Luke's hands. Then he looked at his face, then back to his hands, then at his feet, and finally back to his hands again.

'Jack of all trades, I expect, and master of none.'

Luke said nothing. The two women listened and gazed in silence as though waiting for him to go. And then Thompson, as though in finality too, reached forward and took up the Bible again and held it outstretched, in an attitude of half-dramatic carelessness towards the girl.

'Lily, put the Book away.'

Luke reached the door and had his hand on the knob before Thompson spoke again and before the girl had taken the book.

'Hasty?' he said.

'I don't want to waste your time, that's all.'

'Time is common property,' said Thompson. 'What work have you been doing? Time is a common gift from Almighty God.' He waited a moment. 'Not much, by the look of you.'

'I been knocked up.'

'Tell me what you can do.'

'I'm a shoemaker.'

'A shoemaker?'

It was as though he did not believe it. He spread out his hand and drew it down his face with a gesture of pure sarcasm, as though wiping away a smile.

'What do you think a shoemaker might do on a farm?'

'I'm a tidy hand with a scythe.'

'A lot of mowing to be done in March.'

'All right.'

Luke had taken his hand momentarily off the door knob. He put it back again.

'I didn't ask you to go,' said Thompson. He reached out his right hand to the girl, clicking his thumb against his forefinger imperatively, as though asking for the Bible back again. 'What is the quotation? What is it? "He that refuseth instruction—" How does it go? "He that refuseth—refuseth—"'

No one spoke and Thompson went on, with a kind of sarcastic impatience, exaggerated a little, 'Well? A simple quotation and not one of us can finish it. Well, Mrs. Thompson? Come.'

'It's from the Book of Proverbs,' said the woman.

'The Book of Proverbs,' he said. Thompson looked at the woman impersonally. She was not so tall as he, but she did not look up at him when speaking or listening. She gazed instead straight forward, so that her gaze rested upon his white, foldless collar. She had grey pellucid eyes which were perpetually transfixed, vaguely, in an almost sightless fashion. Standing there, gazing at Thompson's collar with her soft expressionless eyes, she seemed to be physically dead, or if not dead in a dream. She seemed to have gone beyond the effect of all emotion, certainly beyond the effect of Thompson's emotional subtleties, into a world of insensible despondency. Her very immobility and the very senseless and unchanging tone of her voice were full of melancholy.

'I think it is the Book of Proverbs,' she said. Her voice, completely unchanging in tone, was as flat as her stare at Thompson.

'You think,' he said.

'I believe mother is right,' said the girl. She spoke for the first time, her voice with some of the strength of Thompson himself.

'You think, and you believe,' he said. He looked at them, separately at first and then together, with a look of utterly impersonal contempt, his mouth drawn and flattened liplessly into an immovable smile. 'You think and you believe.'

'But you don't know!' he said, raising his voice. 'Turn up the Book of Samuel. The second Book.'

'It's Proverbs,' said the girl.

'I am asking you to turn up the Book of Samuel.'

'Will you begin the quotation again?' she said.

'I will repeat nothing, my dear girl. Turn up the Book of Samuel.'

She resigned. Her lips became almost as flat as Thompson's and almost as emotionless as her mother's. She asked him, in a voice deliberately devoid of emotion, for chapter and verse, and he replied in a voice that might have been the magnified echo of it, an echo of accentuated mockery.

'The second Book of Samuel. The fifth chapter.' He spoke slowly. 'Verse fifteen.'

With the same impersonal and emotionless air as before the girl turned over the leaves of the Bible, pressing them out at last. All the time Thompson stared at her with the same flattened humourless smile which seemed to make his face larger than ever. The woman stared in turn at him, her eyes expressionlessly fixed on the point where his Adam's apple fitted into the angle of his collar. Then when the girl had found the place Thompson spoke. 'Read it,' he said. The girl did not open her mouth.

'Read it,' said Thompson. He looked at Luke. 'I hope you are listening?' he said. 'It is for your good.'

When he had finished speaking the girl's lips relaxed. She began to read out. 'Ibhar also,' she read, 'and Elishua, and—'

'And John the Apostle, you will tell me next.'

She looked at him quietly for a moment before looking back at the book.

'It was the wrong verse.'

'Most curious.'

He waited.

'I am waiting,' he said.

'And Elishama,' she was reading the next verse now, 'and Eliada—'

He reached out his hand coldly and unexcitedly, and took the Bible from her.

'Elishama,' he repeated, 'and Eliada.'

Even the face of the woman underwent a faint change at the bitterness of that contempt. The girl looked at Luke. He felt a violent desire, as he had done with the constables, to smash Thompson in the face, but he was conscious of a curious sickness and impotence also, and he said nothing. And finally Thompson began to read.

'He that refuseth instruction—' he read with slow gravity, with a meticulous and heavy accent, not looking at the Book—'he that refuseth instruction shall be numbered among the foolish, and his children thereafter.'

The girl looked at him all the time with extreme penetration. She was as tall as her mother, but she looked up at Thompson. Her dark brown dress was fastened close up under her neck and she held back her head as though the dress restricted and pained her throat. It gave her a look of extreme pride, her eyes all the time very clear and dispassionately light.

She was still looking at Thompson when he finished reading and when he leaned forward to replace the Bible, closed, upon the table, but he did not look at her in return.

He was looking at Luke instead. 'There is something in that Book to fit every occasion,' he said. 'And every man, woman and child, too, if it comes to that. But you know that already.'

'I ain't much of a Bible-reader.'

'Where do you come from?'

'Nenweald.'

Thompson smiled. 'Nenweald—all hair and teeth, isn't that it? A rough lot.'

Luke did not speak. He could feel the girl looking at him. He felt at the same time a desire to smash Thompson in the face again.

Unexpectedly Thompson spoke once more.

'If I don't find you work I suppose the devil will. You had better come along in the morning.'

Luke stood for a moment looking from Thompson to the girl and then from the girl to the woman, still gazing expressionlessly in front of her. But no one spoke, and finally he said 'Thanks' and opened the door. As he reached the passage outside Thompson called after him:

'Here a moment. You could do worse than take this with you.' He had the Bible in his hands.

'I ain't much of a reader.'

Thompson stretched out his hand.

'Learn,' he said.

Luke took the Bible and went along the passage and let himself out into the yard. It was dark outside except in the extreme west, where the sky was still a pale lemon-colour, clear and cold. The stars were shining, and as he went across the orchard, through the damson trees, he looked back. The blinds in the farmhouse had not been drawn, and he could see Thompson walking up and down in the lamplight, a dominating figure, his big hand raised and lowered as though in explanation of something, and the two women still standing there.

CHAPTER IV

I

He worked at Valley Farm, Thompson's place, as a labourer all that spring. He was seventeen miles from Nenweald; it seemed as though he were in another world. He lodged with the Stricklands. Every morning at four he got up by candlelight in order to be in the farm kitchen by half-past and drink the beer and eat the bread and cheese that the kitchen-girl had set out on the table for himself and his sixteen fellow hands. The farm was very large and of the six hundred acres more than half were arable that year, the meadow-lands lying along the river, at the feet of the gentle slopes on which the house stood. He was at muck-cart during March and the early weeks of April, and the work, at first, almost finished him. He was so weak that in the evenings, sometimes, he could not stand upright. During the day the muck, by a sort of suction, dragged away the strength, down through his arms and hands and even down to his finger-tips. He was glad to lean on the wheels of the carts, surreptitiously, to rest. He had no reserves of strength and endurance. And he was so blindly weary that, going home across the fields at the end of the day, he did not see the first-opened primroses on the copse-edge, and later the dark green spikes of the first bluebells among them. It was not until the end of April, when the weather was warmer and he had begun to get back his strength, that he troubled to think about the spring. He saw it emotionlessly even then. He became fully aware of it only when the damson trees came into blossom at last, in the green orchard. He first saw the trees, consciously, one Sunday morning, as he went back home after helping with the cows. The black trees had changed by a miracle to white. They stood transfigured, the blossom a miracle of whiteness. The half-transparent petals were so light that there was hardly a shadow on the grass. The cowslips had come out too, rich yellow in the white-petalled orchard, and he could see the bees working in them and in the damson trees. Separately, and then together, he could smell the scents of cowslips and grass and damson blossom. It was quiet except for the sound the bees made. And he stood listening to them and watching them and looking at the white blossom and breathing the scent of it all until he could stand no longer.

From somewhere about that time he began to come back to life. He began to like the work and the farm and to be conscious of liking it. The May weather was dry that year and Thompson's corn dark and thick. As he took his place in the hoeing-rows Luke felt a pride in the corn, as though it had been his own. Towards the end of May, before the corn was too high, the docks had to be pulled. The men worked with hooked sticks of ash or hazel, using the hooks to lever under the forks of the dock-roots. The docks had to be up-rooted unbroken, to the last tip of hair-root. And periodically Thompson came into the field in order to watch and see that that was done. He would walk up and down the rows behind the men, watching but not speaking, like a guard in charge of a working party of prisoners. The men were silent too, pulling up the docks and throwing them aside, into the osier corn-skips, without a murmur. Thompson walked only a yard or two behind the men, so that eventually, when a man broke off a dock too short, he would be near enough to kick him in the back.

One afternoon Luke broke a dock short, leaving the root half in the earth, and Thompson, standing just behind, kicked him. Luke fell heavily on his knees and hands among the corn. The blow from Thompson's foot seemed terrific and for a moment or two he could not get up. While he lay there Thompson kicked him again.

'Get up,' he said, 'can't you!'

Luke got up. He was dazed and could not see Thompson clearly.

'Get it out clean,' said Thompson.

Luke looked round for his stick.

'Get it out,' Thompson repeated.

The stick lay a yard or two up the rows and as Luke bent forward to pick it up Thompson aimed another kick at him.

'Now get it up,' he said.

Luke half-knelt among the corn and began to uproot the dock again, his back turned away from Thompson. He felt curiously weak, submissive. The kick had knocked the spirit out of him. He worked at the dock mechanically, conscious of nothing but the pain in his buttocks and his fear of Thompson standing over him. He scratched the dry earth with his hands, like a dog, in order to find where the root had broken off, yellow, under the surface. All the time Thompson stood over him, saying nothing. It was only when the thin spear of dock-root had been pulled out that Thompson spoke again.

'Now you know,' he said.

Luke said nothing.

'Don't you? Answer me.'

'Yes.'

'Then take care you don't forget.'

Thompson walked away up the wheat-rows, and then hesitated and then came back.

'See me when you leave off.'

In the evening, when he went to the house, Luke could

still feel the ache at the foot of his spine where Thompson had kicked him. He stood in the kitchen while the girl told Thompson he was there. Presently when the girl came back Thompson was with her, but the girl disappeared as soon as she opened the door. Thompson looked at Luke and spoke:

'I want to give you a chance,' he said.

Luke said nothing; he felt instinctively that Thompson expected him to say nothing.

'What were you,' Thompson went on, 'before you came here?'

'I told you. A shoemaker.'

'A shoemaker.'

It was the old habit of contemptuous repetition and Thompson paused to allow the effect of it to pass before he spoke again.

'You can mend boots?' he said.

'Yes.'

'Any boots?'

'Yes.'

Thompson looked at his own feet. 'These boots?' he said. The boots were black, of hard kip-leather that would not shine, and the soles were double thickness, the caps broad and powerful.

'Yes,' Luke said.

'They're my preaching boots,' said Thompson.

'They're heavy.'

'They need to be heavy,' said Thompson, 'since I walk twenty miles in them every Sunday. Twenty miles on Sunday and ten every Tuesday. They need to be heavy.'

Suddenly Thompson sat down in a chair and began to take off the boots. As he pulled them off and set them on the brick floor they seemed larger than ever. 'I want to give you a chance,' he said. He picked up the boots together in one hand. 'You say you can mend them?'

'Yes.'

'Don't say you can if you can't. Look at them. Take a good look at them.'

Luke picked up the boots. They were hot and moist inside from the sweat of Thompson's feet and they were a dead weight in his hands. He turned them over and looked at them. The soles were whitish and worn already by the summer roads, and the heels were rounded down by the repeated force of Thompson's step.

Luke put the boots down on the kitchen floor again.

'I could mend them,' he said.

'Then mend them.'

'When?' said Luke.

'I want them before Sunday.'

'I got no tools,' Luke said.

'That's nothing to do with me,' said Thompson. 'Get some.'

He was out of the room before Luke could speak again, calling, 'Lily, Lily, where are you? Where are my slippers?' as he strode softly down the passage in his stockinged feet.

2

Luke borrowed fifteen shillings, all Strickland could spare him, and walked the seven miles into Bedford on the following evening and bought the tools he knew he would need. It was twilight before he was back at Strickland's again. Then he sat in the kitchen, handicapped by having no bench, and worked with the shoe-last between his knees, by candlelight, stripping off the old soles and the worn heel-lifts, studding the new with the same kind of square-headed pins that Thompson had worn down to mere shavings of silver in the old. It was midnight before he had finished. In the morning he was at the house before six o'clock. Thompson himself met him at the door. Thompson looked at the boots and took them without a word, only turning them over in his hand. He was already dressed for preaching. His black cloth suit heightened the fiery colour of his hair. Looking at the boots he murmured with a kind of savage rumination about something before slamming the door. An hour later, when Luke saw him striding down the road by Strickland's, he had a large Bible in one hand, and an ash-stick in the other.

In the afternoon, as Luke was coming across the cow-yard with the first milk-buckets, Lily Thompson called him to the house.

'My shoes want mending,' she said.

Standing with the milk-buckets in his hands, he said nothing; he did not know what to say.

'I saw the boots you mended for father,' she went on.

He spoke abruptly with his old tone of laconic irony. 'I dare say,' he said.

'He says you're to mend them.'

'All right, if he says so.'

'He did say so.'

'All right.'

He looked instantly down at her boots. They were black and rather slender-toed, with high uppers that buttoned up. He could see that they were quite elegant, the calf leather soft and smooth and fitting rather tightly to her feet.

'You ain't very hard on 'em,' he said.

'They want mending,' she said.

'Let's look. Hold up.'

'I'll take them off if you like,' she said.

'All right. Take it off.'

She sat down on the kitchen steps and began to un-button her boot. Waiting, he set down the milk-buckets, and finally, when she gave him the boot, he turned it over and over in his hand, critically. The sole of the boot was sound, and along the edge of it the leather was still a light corn-colour as though she had hardly worn the boots.

'They're good,' he said.

'But they want mending,' she said. 'Don't they?'

He gave the boot back to her, sole uppermost. She turned it over quickly and put it on and began to button it up again.

'You'll go a tidy way in 'em yet,' he said.

'They hurt me,' she said.

'I dare say.'

He waited till she had buttoned up the boot before he picked up the milk-buckets and walked away. She called after him as he walked across the yard and he turned and promised to mend the boots.

In the evening she called at the Stricklands' and asked for him. He had gone into her father's meadows to fish for an hour, but the Stricklands told her where to find him, and she walked across the meadows of mown hay to where he was worm-fishing under a line of alders. She had the boots tied up in brown paper. He did not hear her coming and he was on his feet, ready to run, before he knew who it was, and she gave an exclamation of surprise as though she had not seen him either. In a moment he sat down on the river bank again and she sat down too, saying she had brought the boots. He said nothing. In the quietness over the river there was hardly a sound except the motion of the grasshoppers in the uncut fringe of grass. Out in the stream his cork float, home-made, with its white hen's feather, was motionless. He was really not fishing, only passing the time and trying to feel the stream. Then as he sat there, silent, watching the river, she said for the second time that she had brought the boots.

Not knowing what to say, he kept silent. It was almost a year since he had fished. He had no rod and was using a willow-branch, with the line tied to the end, as he had done when a boy. The stream was placid, deep and so slow that the float hardly moved, and when she asked if he had caught anything he shook his head.

A moment later his float jerked and sank. He struck, amused to see the little roach that came up frenziedly struggling on a hook. He brought the roach to the bank and took the hook from its mouth. The fish slipped from his hand and began to slap about on the bank before he could catch it again.

Lily Thompson began to laugh as the roach danced on the bank and he stared in astonishment at the sudden sound of her voice. It was very rich and full of pleasure. He saw that she was standing up and that she was half-dancing too with the pleasure that the dancing roach gave her. Every time the roach leaped and squirmed her voice took on fresh tones of delight. 'Don't touch it, don't touch it,' she kept saying. 'Don't touch it!' The roach leapt and squirmed vainly in the grass and Lily drank in eagerly every movement of its struggles. His hand closed over it at last, its little dark mouth panting open and shut in rapid gasps. 'You're not to throw it back!' she said. 'You're not to.'

'Why?' he said. 'Why not?'

'I want to see it, I want to see it!'

He threw the roach down in the grass and after it had struggled for a moment or two she seized it in her hands, as he had done, so that its mouth gasped open and shut in rapid agony between her thumb and forefinger. He kept telling her to throw the roach into the water again, but by the time she had ceased laughing at its suffering the roach was dead.

After that he untied his line and threw the willow-rod into the grass and they walked back up the hay-meadows again. Lily still carried her shoes. The weather was very dry and the hay, lying still unturned in the long curved swathes where the scythers had left it, was almost white in the evening sunshine. They walked slowly across the swathes, hardly speaking. Then, coming up the last meadow by the hedgeside, they saw Thompson walking along the road above them. They could see nothing but his black square hat above the hedgerow and they watched it until it had disappeared.

'He's late coming back,' Luke said.

'No. This is his time. Somewhere about eight o'clock.'

He wanted to know how far he walked each Sunday, and she said:

'Twenty miles. Perhaps more.'

'Just to preach? Why don't he take the trap?'

'He says it's his duty to walk on the feet God gave him. When I was a child I went with him.'

She talked in a curiously flat voice, unamazed, and he said:

'Why don't you go with him now?'

'I'm twenty-two,' she said. 'I can do what I like.'

'Ah!'

'Almost. He's not my father at all.'

She spoke all the time in the same flat, cold voice, quite impersonally, as though she despised Thompson. Finally she made a sound of impatience, a slight 'Oh!' as though she did not want to talk of him at all.

Out of the meadow, in the road, by Strickland's place, he left her. The white pinks were in bloom in Strickland's garden, the evening air heavily sweet with their fragrance, and as he stood breathing it in he suddenly wondered why she had not given him the boots after all.

CHAPTER V

I

AFTER that, quite suddenly and for no reason, he began to like her. She seemed nearly always to be about the farmyard whenever he walked across with the pig-buckets or a load of straw, and he began to look forward to seeing her, in the white big-sleeved dress that she wore, and then to be disappointed when she was not there. He hardly ever spoke to her during the daytime. But seeing him, she would stand still and smile, or when she was too far away she would lift her hand in a half-secret gesture of friendliness. Unlike the women on the farms he had always known she and Mrs. Thompson did no work. Mrs. Thompson, very frail and subdued, would sit sewing under the damson trees in the fine summer mornings, and in the afternoon Lily would join her. If he were working on that side of the house he could see the two women as they sat there; two white figures under the dark green trees, motionless except for the infinitely brief movements of their hands as they sewed or the slow white flutter of the pages if Lily were reading. They were symbols of a genteel and leisurely life he had hardly believed could exist. And after a time he began to see why Lily's boots were scarcely worn. Except for the walk into the orchard Mrs. Thompson scarcely walked at all. Every journey made beyond the white gates that opened on to the road at the end of the house-drive was made either in the trap, if Thompson were with her, or in the buggy if she and Lily went alone. And they were the only excursions he could see that either she or Lily made. At first they seemed to be bound to the house. Then he saw that they were bound not so much to the house as to Thompson. As she sat in the orchard Mrs. Thompson would keep her eyes half-averted towards the fields, as though consciously or unconsciously watching for Thompson to come. Whenever he did come she would drop her sewing and sometimes rise to her feet; if she did not get up she would sit with her hands on the chair-arms, in suspense, only relaxing if by some chance Thompson went out of sight again. She sat in a kind of subservient terror. Lily did nothing. She never rose when Thompson appeared, never even looked up from her book. She sat in unspoken contempt, just as her mother sat in unspoken fear and obedience. She read a great deal: large volumes, with pink marbled edges, which at some time Thompson had had bound up in plain calf, uniformly, so that it seemed as though she were for ever reading the same book and never coming to the end.

It was a book which made her go to the Stricklands' one evening, asking for Luke. She carried the book as she had done her shoes, wrapped in brown paper. When she un-wrapped it he saw that the book was split down the spine. She had thrown it at the cat. He wanted to know why. She said, 'I wanted to, that's all. I just wanted to.' He stood fingering the smooth calf, with pleasure, as she asked him to repair it. The book was Scott's *Bride of Lammermoor* and before he could speak again she asked him if he had read it.

'I only read one book in my life,' he said. 'That was *Martyrs*. Fox's *Martyrs*.'

'I love that,' she said. 'Oh! I love that. But you should read Scott. He's romantic. *Kenilworth*—you'd like that. I've read all Scott—all the tales and the poems.'

It was beyond him; he tried to say once that he would glue the torn calf, but she took no notice, going on to tell him of what she had read and not read and what she longed to read.

'Why don't you read?' she said.

'Never had time.'

'But why? Why?'

'I had summat else to do.'

He was embarrassed and she revelled in his embarrassment, catechizing him continually until he told her at last:

'I was too busy doing what I was told.'

'And what was that?'

He did not answer. They were standing at the gate of Strickland's little farmyard, and suddenly, as she spoke, it all came back to him as he had first seen it. The hen-yard under the snow, the frightened hens, the woman with the steaming hen-mash, her cries, his own fear. It was the persistence of his own fear which made him say:

'I'll tell you some time.'

But she was not satisfied, and she kept up her persistent questioning until he was half-desperate, the poaching days, the murder and the death of his father all coming back to him again and again. And then, as his desperation reached its height and he was ready and even anxious, for the pure relief of it, to tell her everything, her voice lost its insistent intensity, she gave him a brief smile of assurance and she seemed to give it up.

'I'll tell you some time,' he said.

And strangely, she seemed content with that, giving him a brief smile of reassurance, as though she were half-sorry and as though she half-understood.

Soon afterwards Thompson asked him if he could make

him a pair of boots. 'If you make them well I might get you
to make a pair for Mrs. Thompson, and then one for Lily.'

'I shall have to measure you, and get lasts.'

'Very well. Get the lasts. You can drive into market with
me to-morrow.'

He finished the boots for Thompson by the end of the
next week. They were of the same funereal, unshining black
kip-leather as the preaching boots and Thompson took them
and turned them over and over in his hands without comment. Luke stood waiting and finally Thompson said:

'How much, then, am I in your debt?'

'A pound and sixpence, counting the lasts.'

'The lasts!' Thompson said. 'What are the lasts to do with
me?'

'I had to get them.'

'You had to get them.' Thompson said. He paused. 'Do
they belong to me or to you?'

'They're mine.'

'They're yours and yet you want to charge me for them.'

'It's expenses.'

'If you pay for the lasts, they're yours,' said Thompson
slowly. 'If I pay for them, it's expenses.'

'I don't reckon you twig it, quite. It's understood.'

'Understood? I don't understand. What do the lasts cost
you?'

'Four-and-six.'

Thompson took out his purse, a silver-ringed bag of soft
leather, and counted out sixteen shillings and laid the
money on the table of the room where he did his accounts.
Luke did not pick the money up and Thompson said:

'Isn't that right?'

Luke did not answer and Thompson began very slowly,
shilling by shilling, to pick up the money and put it back into
his purse again.

'We must come to a different arrangement, then, if it isn't
right.'

'I said a pound and sixpence.'

'We must come to a different arrangement.'

Standing rigid, angry more even with himself than with Thompson, Luke hardly listened as Thompson went on to tell him how, in future, he would make the boots and mend them in Thompson's time and not his own. 'Whatever tools you want, then, I will buy. You can fill in your time with the harness.' He wanted to say something about the gross injustice of Thompson's behaviour, but Thompson stood looking at him with an expression of fixed contempt, his lips pursed into a flat half-smile, and finally Luke picked up his cap and went out of the room without a word.

From that day he began to spend his time making and mending shoes for the Thompson family and repairing the harness and saddlery; he worked at a bench which Thompson allowed him to put up in an old wash-house behind the stables, out of sight of the house and the orchard. Thompson wore out his boots quickly, more than thirty horses were at work on the farm, and there was always work for him to do. Gradually the new clean wood of the bench became leather-stained and littered with leather-skivings and tacks and pins and rivets of steel and brass, and the many files and hammers and awls and pincers of his craft, and the place full of the acrid odours of new leather and the stink of the hot wax-pot. And gradually also, as the first sense of restlessness subdued itself, he liked working there. He liked the feeling of solitude and serenity that came of being alone. There was a little window in the place. He could look over the fields, across the valley, as he had done with his father at Nenweald. And once, as he sat there thinking of his father, he picked up a piece of wire from the bench and twisted it half-consciously into a circle and then into a snare. He put the wire down on the bench without thinking what he had done and it lay there for a week without his noticing it again. One day when Lily came in to bring a pair of her boots the snare was still lying on the bench. She saw it and picked it up and ran the noose together, until it almost closed. He took it away from her and put it down on the bench. She took it up again. She wanted to know what it was. He said: 'A noose.' She looked as if she did not understand. He said: 'A snare, if you like, a trap.' She kept running the noose in and out, over her fingers. 'What for?' she asked. He said: 'For rats. I got rats all under this bench.' After that she scarcely spoke about the snare again and he forgot it as he worked and talked with her. It was only when she was outside the door that it occurred to him that she still had the snare in her hand.

He called her back, then, and dragged her inside the workshop and took the snare away from her before she had time to speak. He was trembling with sudden agitation. She stared at him with a kind of thrilled astonishment as he threw the snare under the bench.

'What's the matter?' she said.

'It's a rabbit snare. I thought you twigged that.'

'What if it is?'

'D'ye want to get me *hung*?' he said. 'I could get gaoled for even making that.'

She stood listening with a curious eagerness, with a strange look of half-scared delight on her face, as though his words thrilled and frightened her. And, as he clenched the wire in his hands, screwing it up to a meaningless knot, he saw the look on her face, misinterpreting it as a horror of himself.

He said at once: 'It's all right. I didn't want Thompson— I didn't want your father to know, that's all.' He threw the wire under the bench. 'If he knew about that wire he'd smash me.'

'Smash you?'

'Y' understand, don't you? It's agin the law.'

'Then why did you make it?'

'It was an accident. I didn't know I was making it.'

She paused before speaking again. A strange expression had come over her face, a look of vivid contempt, and when she spoke she was very excited.

'As if I would have told him. Him!'

Before he had time to speak she went on, the contempt if anything increasing, her face almost white in its anger.

'And don't call him my father! He isn't my father.'

He tried to murmur something apologetic, in explanation, but she had gone before he could recover himself from his profound surprise. It was not until afterwards that he discovered that he was trembling too.

2

They began to be drawn together, from about that time, by a common hatred of Thompson. It became so that whenever he expected to see her he found himself searching his mind for some incident, even a sentence or a word, expressive of Thompson's meanness or hypocrisy. It was almost harvest, and Thompson had still not paid him for the shoes he had made him in the early summer. They talked of it for days, the sum of Thompson's ingratitude accumulating, as it were, an interest of bitterness whenever they spoke of it. They gained a strange pleasure from that secret and combined hatred. It even became so that he did not want Thompson to pay him for the shoes so that the pleasure of their mutual emotion might still go on. And as though she saw that too she said: 'I wouldn't take the money now, if he were to offer it.' He said he wouldn't be seen dead with the money. Not if Thompson went down on his bended knees. He told her also of the day Thompson had kicked him in the field. She in return would tell him of happenings in the house, little incidents of persecution as regular and habitual with him as the morning or evening prayers, of how Thompson would persecute her indirectly, through Mrs. Thompson, her own mother. They talked of the first night Luke had come into the house, and she told him of what he did not know, but had half-suspected, of how Thompson, mistaken in the chapter and verse of his text, had made up the words.

They went on from mutual hatred of Thompson to a kind of reticent, unspoken anxiety for each other, and from that into confidences and for some time an unspoken admiration and tenderness. He told her a good deal about his life, about the running and the poaching, the hand-to-

121

mouth way he had always lived, his aunt and the reading, the death of his father, and at last, sure of her confidence, about the murder and all the folly of his escape in the snow. He felt strangely relieved and at rest when he had told her everything. It was a refreshing sensation. His fears and even the shame he still felt at his own foolishness seemed nothing. Having told her everything, he could not think why he had ever been afraid or foolish or ashamed.

One day, in the workshop, as they were bending over the bench looking for a needle he had dropped among his tacks and pins, he put his arm round her shoulder and let his hand run across her neck before he began kissing her. It let loose in her a flood of unexpected passion. He felt her trembling. As she uprighted herself he slipped his hands down from her shoulders to take her by the waist, his hands running down over her tightened breasts half-accidentally. She seemed to come to life at once. He kissed her again. Trembling violently, she held herself very close to him, her body hardened, in an effort to quieten herself. She did not speak except to ask him to kiss her again. When he had done that she seemed to be trembling more violently than ever. He could not hold her still.

After that they gave up meeting in the workshop. It was not enough for her to be in love; the love must also be romantic. So they began to meet in a wood that bounded the Thompson land on the south side. And when they met there, after twilight, after he had finished the overtime he was working in the harvest field, the meeting was everything to her by its secrecy. Her emotions were heightened by an everlasting fear of discovery.

It filled all their time together with a kind of ecstatic anxiety. Sometimes he could not get to the wood until ten at night. But however late he was she would be there waiting. She whipped up her expectancy at his coming and her fear that he was not coming into a sort of ecstatic fever. When he finally came, already tired out by the harvest-field, she exhausted him utterly by the intensity of her talking. He never fully understood it all. He did not know what to think of her. He had never heard anyone talk as she talked. At first it was like a romantic gibberish. It was something quite remote from his own shifty though prosaic life. It was not enough for her that he should make love to her simply. It had to be done romantically, strangely, as though he were a character out of one of her impossible novels. 'Kiss me, kiss me. I shall swoon. Kiss me.' The silliness of her dreary voice, so unlike the rather correct, clipped speech of her normal life, at first tortured him. Gradually he got used to it, gave himself up to it, and then did not think of it. He knew at last what she wanted. And it was only when she began to love him physically, giving herself night after night in the wood with an ease that astounded him, that she ceased to trouble about loving him romantically. She no longer spoke the strange, silly language which had so bewildered him. She scarcely spoke at all. She loved him in an almost complete silence of elation. He understood her then.

If there was any talking at all, then, it was he who did it. Lily was pretty in a pale, rather hard way, her grey eyes cold and light, like water. He thought she was very lovely, and she seemed to him to grow more lovely as the days went past and his tenderness increased.

'Ah, ye're my treasure,' he would say. 'Ain't you? Ye're my treasure?'

'You know best about that.'

'Yes, ye'are. Ye're my treasure. Ye're my treasure.'

It was not until after harvest, when the stubbles were empty, cleaned even of their gleanings under the softly remote September skies, that there was another change in her. She was almost sure by then that she was going to have a child.

3

To his astonishment she was not troubled. It was almost as if she had set out, deliberately, to have the child, knowing that if she succeeded there could only be one solution to it

123

all—to escape from the farm. He knew that that had been her ambition for a long time and it did not surprise him when, at the beginning of October, she told him that she was certain of the child and that they must get away. She seemed eager to go away at once, excitedly eager, half as though it were not only imperative but a little romantic to be running away with him in secret. He, in turn, knowing that it was the only possible thing, was troubled only by where they should go.

'We'll go back to where you came from,' she said.

'Nenweald!'

'Can you think of anywhere else?' she said.

She was imperative, and it was she who made the plans for their going, just as she had made the plans for meeting in the wood. What she said was final, unanswerable. He could do nothing. She had one unassailable answer to whatever he might think or say:

'Can you think what would happen if we stayed *here*?'

Finally, towards the middle of October, they went. It was very simple. It was easy to arrange one afternoon that Lily should go into Bedford on a shopping errand and almost as easy to arrange that he should drive and that they should not come back again. It all passed off simply and easily, without any unusual happening except a very brief one which he never forgot; and this was when Lily, asking him to stop the trap before they had gone half a mile, turned in her seat and slowly and with a kind of vicious premeditation, spat in the direction of the farm.

They arrived in Nenweald late in the afternoon. The sight of the familiar spire, the houses, the Square with the flourishing chestnut trees planted to commemorate the accession of the Queen, filled him with a strange sense of foreboding and pleasure. He knew that there was only one thing for him to do and only one person for him to see.

He sat with his aunt for almost an hour. For once she scarcely spoke. It was only when he had said all he had to say that she came out of her silence.

'It's a good job,' she said then, 'it's nothing worse. I

thought you'd been jabey enough to go off for a soldier.' And at last, 'Where's the girl?'

'Outside.'

'Fetch her in then.'

When he went out of the house to find Lily it was almost dark, and the wind, blowing in a north-easterly direction from over the river, was bringing with it brief gusts of rain that surprised him with their bitterness.

It was only then that he realized, for the first time, that it was almost winter.

PART THREE: THE LAND

CHAPTER I

I

THEY were married, his aunt lent him twenty pounds, and in the early winter of that year, at her suggestion, he rented a piece of land on the eastern outskirts of the town from a Nenweald baker. He began almost at once to break it up, at first by hand, and then with a light one-horse plough, hiring the plough from a blacksmith and the horse from the baker. There was no house on the land. He and Lily lived in a new red-brick house in one of the rows that were springing up on the edges of Nenweald. Machinery was beginning to come in, factories like tall brick and slate boxes, with thick glass windows, were springing up among the houses, and the town was expanding. Everywhere there was talk of development; the railway was coming; great changes, people declared, were going to happen in the order of things. Already it was becoming apparent in the wage disputes, the black-aproned shoemakers arguing at the factory corners in the dinner-hours, the hammer and whine of new machinery, strikes, politicians spouting on the Square in the evenings, echoing the thunder of Bradlaugh. Religion was coming in with the machines; little chapels of corrugated iron and raw brick were springing up, indistinguishable at a distance from the factories and the tanning-sheds; and with it all the speculator in property, the temperance reformer, and the rise of a new class, the working-class, as distinct from the labourers and the old shoemakers working by hand, independently.

But working on his piece of land, alone, Luke scarcely noticed it. In the shortening winter days he worked all day, from dark to dark, eating his midday meals in the ditch, under the hedge. He had no time to think of any outside life. At times, if the wind sat right, he could hear the sound of the river-digger, the great American steam implement cutting the course for the railway. He would lean on his spade or on the plough-handles and listen to it. An incredible implement, moving more earth in one movement than he himself could move in a day. He listened to it vaguely; it meant nothing to him. Similarly the life of the past began to recede and mean nothing, as having no part in the breaking up of his new soil. He ceased even to trouble, as he had troubled at first, about Thompson and the possibility of his pursuit and proceedings. Life was translated into terms of soil; the turning-over of soil, the breaking-up of it, the sight of it, its wet, wintry smell. He tasted soil in his bread; it began to be so deeply ditched in his hands that he could never wash it out.

His field was almost square, with a northward slope, and in all about five acres. At the end of two months he had broken up a strip about twenty yards wide and going the full length of it. On a November afternoon he sowed his first wheat on it, broadcast. Snow fell soon afterwards. When it had vanished he could see the first shoots of his wheat, miraculously green on the snow-levelled land. It seemed wonderful. The next day he urged Lily to walk up to the field and look at it. She was in her fourth month. She was wearing tight stays and the walk exhausted her. When she arrived at the field she wanted to do nothing but sit down and rest. She had not the strength to look at the wheat. There was nowhere for her to sit except the ground. So he spread out a sack for her, and then his jacket over the sack.

'It's time you had a hut or a hovel or something, where you could shelter,' she said.

So in the new year he began to put up the first buildings, a wooden hut for his tools and a sty for his first pig. The hut was very small, but he built it under the shelter of the high hawthorn hedge, with a little window facing south, and it seemed like a sanctuary after the wintry bitterness of the bare land.

'You could come up there, fine afternoons,' he said to Lily, 'and keep me company.'

'I don't want to come.'

He thought she seemed wretched. He put it down to the child.

'You're all right, ain't you?' he said.

'I'm all right.'

'You got to get out more.'

'I don't want to go out. Where could I go if I went out?'

'You could go and see my mother.'

'Your mother?'

It was as though, unconsciously, she had picked up that trick of ironical repetition from Thompson. He said nothing. He knew that, except for one single occasion. Lily had never been to see his mother, and that ever since, as though in retaliation, neither his mother nor his sisters had called on him. He had not time to consider the intricacies of feminine jealousy. But vaguely, mutely, he was hurt and could not forget it all.

Nevertheless all that winter he cherished a constant and tender adoration for her. He knew, vaguely, without ever analysing himself very deeply, that he himself had changed; he had grown quieter. The death of his father, the murder, the brief period of subjection to Thompson had chastened him. Looking back, he could regard with nothing but astonishment the old life, the night after night poaching, the risks and the fears. He could hardly believe he had taken part in it. He was so concerned now with the land, with Lily and with the coming of the child that he could not believe he had ever been concerned with other things.

Towards the end of the winter, when the days began to lengthen, he found himself looking ahead. He had by that time broken up a little more than half the field. It was ungracious land, a heavyish clay. In the spring winds the earth dried out into harsh clots which, by great labour, he broke down with a clot-hoe. Looking ahead, he laid his plans for the field; how, that summer, he would have, besides his wheat, a strip of oats and another of barley; and then a patch of potatoes, then some swedes and some cabbages, leaving a strip of grass the whole length of the field. Then, if things turned out well, he could graze a horse or a cow. He had no illusions as to how far he might go or how much he might do. His strength and his ambitions were both limitless. His strength came back to him fully with the sun, so that, as the light of the year increased, his own energy increased too. He did nothing but work. For a period, during the coincident planting of potatoes and barley, he did not go into the streets of Nenweald except once. He went then to get his hair cut, and, worn out, fell asleep in the barber's chair. At night, in his sleep, he re-enacted all he had done during the day, opening endless trenches in the spring earth in order to plant in them everlasting lines of potatoes. Working single-handed, he found himself working unceasingly against time. He got up at daybreak, came downstairs in his shirt, lighted the fire, went back to dress, and then, coming down again without waking Lily, ate his breakfast standing up. During the night he would wake recurrently, afraid that he would oversleep himself. Then he took enough bread and bacon into the field with him for the day. On fine days he sat under the hedge to eat. But if it were wet or cold he would sit in the tool-hut, staring at the field through the already cob-webbed window, making fresh plans and criticizing, half-unconsciously, those he had already made. There were many things that he wanted: a horse and cart, a plough, a harrow, a cow, some hens, an infinite catalogue of live and dead stock. A horse would mean a stable, the hens a fowl-house. And he wondered sometimes which he should get first, the stable or the horse, the hens or the house, arguing for one side and then another until he saved himself from utter desperation by his own irony and humour:

'Don't know about a horse. Strikes me we'll be lucky if we ever get as far as the halter.'

That spring, just before Lily's confinement, he did not know where to turn for money. They had existed during the winter on the twenty pounds his aunt had lent him and on a little money that Lily had brought from home. He was worried, not for himself, but for Lily, accustomed for so long to the good living of the Thompson household. He was oppressed, too, by the thought of the birth, by the fear that something might happen to Lily. He thought of it in the field, only comforting himself by the thought of a son, thinking of how the son would grow up and help him on the land and be a credit and a comfort to him. Worried by the money, he went to see his aunt. She lent him another twenty pounds, gave him a glass of wine, and discoursed as he had never heard anyone but his father discourse on the great future that was to be for small, one-man holdings such as his own. 'I shan't see it, but you will. When the railway comes you'll be able to put your stuff in the train in the morning and know it'll be in London during the afternoon. And perhaps eaten before night. I know what I'm talking about. In a year or two, if you're sharp, you'll be making money.'

Warmed by the wine and impressed and excited by her words, he stayed talking longer than he had intended. When he arrived back home, just after ten o'clock, Lily was in great pain.

Towards morning the child was born. It was a girl. As he walked up the deserted road to the field in the early daylight, he felt as though he had invested his money in something and had been cheated. 'What use is a gal?' he kept thinking. 'God a'mighty, what use is a gal to me?'

2

Already, by the end of the summer, a small farmyard had sprung up in the corner of the field: a ring of hovels and sties, with a copper-house for boiling the winter pig-potatoes, and a stack of hay gathered from the remaining strip of grassland. By August the corn was golden and resplendent, the ears sun-bleached and heavy, the oats pinkish and trembling in the hot breeze. From the beginning of the month he mowed and bonded the successive crops with a labour that only broke off when he ate and slept. The oats first, then the white-eared wheat, and at last, at the beginning of September, the barley. He was a good mower, easy, long-winded. Yet there were times when he thought it would almost kill him when he would straighten his back and gaze up and suddenly see the whole world of stubble and corn and shocks revolving dizzily in a kind of momentary faintness. He worked alone, without help. He had cherished a hope of some help from Lily, but it never came. Almost every day she would come up to the field with the baby, but never to work. Once he suggested it, taking the wheat-straws and showing her how to knot the bonds and tie the sheaves. It was beyond her. She could not see it. And he went over the demonstration again, slowly, and then again, more slowly, twisting the ears together with accentuated simplicity, but without effect. She tried for a little while, but the sheaves, when he picked them up, came untied, and she gave it up. He never mentioned it again. And she would sit all day under a shock or in the shade of the hovel, suckling the child or playing with the pink and white trumpets of convolvulus flowers or, more often, reading. Some sunflower seeds which she had sown by the hut had grown up taller than the corn, with great sun-blossoms, and she liked to sit by them, reading or staring across the field into space, or watching the flowers revolve with the sun. And he, from the field, would look up, and gaze at her, and wonder what she was thinking and what world she lived in.

And gradually, almost without thinking, he began to see that it was not his own world, and that the land meant nothing to her. It was as though, by years of living close to it and yet never on it, she had grown indifferent to it. She had never worked. In thinking of her he would think automatically of his mother, would see her with leather-coloured arms binding endless sheaves or shocking them or gleaning across the empty field, sweating and desperately pushing her straggling gipsyish hair out of her sun-squinted eyes. And then he would see Lily, living in a different world, a world of romantic indolence that he could never fathom, with a child that he scarcely felt was his own.

But strangely, though she never worked, she was ambitious for him. She wanted him to succeed. The labour of turning the bare land to crops, of making the earth flower and yield, was a sort of romantic miracle to her. She loved it, in silence and without expressing it, so long as she never took part in it. It was as if there was no need for her to work. She could accomplish all she wished by dreams, without sweat or pain. And as she sat in the yard, under the haystack or by the sunflowers, she would dream and change it all: change the little ramshackle farmyard to one stretching over half the field, the field itself to twenty, the solitary scythe to many binders. She would dream it until, sometimes, it became an actuality in her own mind. They were rich, they had a carriage and pair, their fields were teeming with cattle and corn. And having made that world, she would live in it, and then dream of a world of even finer and more luxurious achievement beyond it, and then live in that, dreaming of another and more impossibly lovely world still farther beyond.

Thus, though she never worked, it was she in a sense who kept both him and the field alive. Her ambition was the spirit behind all he did. She was never satisfied by the present, by things as they were. She wanted perpetually to be going forward, into the unknown and inevitably romantic future. So, towards the end of harvest, when he was faced with the problem of carting and stacking his corn, it was she who urged him to buy a cart and horse, as though it were the first step towards the carriage and pair of her imagination. He was hesitant, frightened by an expense he could not see his way to meet. And it was she who went to an Orcester brewer, in her maiden name, and bargained with him to make an offer for the barley as it stood. With the promise of that money he bought the horse he had often borrowed from the baker, and a black low-springed cart on two wheels from some travelling gipsies. It was Lily who painted his name on the cart: 'Luke Bishop, Hawthorn Farm, Nenweald,' in white letters, with flourishes, in the face of his amusement and embarrassment at the high-sounding name. 'Hawthorn Farm!' he said. 'There's a lot o' hawthorn—but not much farm.' She was indignant. 'But there *will* be,' she insisted. 'There *will* be.' She almost made him believe in her dream of what the place would be.

Later, when the harvest was over, she urged him to build a stable. She made the plans herself, while he went down with the cart to Nenweald and bought up loads of disused cheap packing cases. Her plans were almost ludicrous; it was as though she wanted to create room not for the horse they did possess but for all the horses they might possess in years to come. And when by the end of October the stable was finished it was utterly unlike the place she had planned. Expense and time and labour had killed her romantic notions one by one. The stable was a square shed built with sections of many packing cases tarred black, with an iron roof and a rough brick floor. It was just large enough for two horses, but it was so low that Luke was forced to stoop inside it. There was no ventilation, so that the stench of urine and urine-sodden hay hung about it thickly, unable to escape. Yet Lily never saw in it anything but the place of her own conception, the spacious stable for many horses. She never saw it with her physical, mortal eyes, but only with the glorifying eyes of her imagination and her dreams. She was not even content with calling it the stable. To her it was always in the plural, the poetic plural. The stables! And she would say it with her rather clipped, haughty accent, so different from his own droll and laconic speech, so that the word took on even finer and more aristocratic shades of meaning.

From the very earliest she began to teach the child her own ways. As with the stable and the field she saw not the child of the present, but of the distant future. She saw it grown up, a beautiful and sensational creature. In her imagination she lived over the love affairs it would have, grand, impossible romances into which she put all the feeling she herself had known and all that she had ever wanted to know. It was a kind of game played in the recesses of her mind, tenderly and ridiculously.

'You got big ideas for that gal,' he would say, 'ain't ye?'

'For Lizzie? Oh! There's no telling what she will be! There's no *telling*.'

He never interfered with her or with the child. He saw them, from the earliest, growing up together. Slaving from morning to dark in the field, he had only time to marvel at it all. It struck him as odd that he had married her, that the child was his, that life had changed. He had no time to go any deeper than that.

After another winter and another spring things began to look up. He had broken up by that time all but a narrow strip of the land. And on the arable section he was growing, on his aunt's advice, more vegetable produce, roots and potatoes and cabbages, with plots of lettuce and radish and peas and beans. In the growing town more and more shops were opening up. He began to supply them. He bought a score of fowls. In the spring and summer he would set off twice a week with the little cart piled high with eggs and vegetables, sheaves of carrots, sacks of cabbages, skips of potatoes, with the eggs lying brown and white in boxes of sweet hay. In a small way he was successful. He was astonished at himself. He found it necessary to begin to keep accounts; it was no longer enough to put the money in a sugar basin in a cupboard; and since he could do very little more than sign his name it was Lily who kept the accounts, dreaming over the figures, magnifying them to impossible proportions. It was she who also urged him to buy the larger cart in time for harvest and to plant the bushes of gooseberry and red and white currant and the trees of apple and plum at the end of the year.

He was occupied during almost the whole month of December with the planting of the trees. He fenced off a section of land just below the farmyard and planted the trees in lines, the gooseberries and currants close together between the taller trees. It was pleasant work; he could take his time; he was his own master. And when the work was finished he was filled with great satisfaction. He would stand and look at the little white tree labels fluttering in the winter wind and at the bare grey branches swaying slightly against the winter sky. It was Christmas by the time he had finished: On Christmas Eve Lily balanced up the accounts. On the year's working they were twenty pounds to the good, not counting their profit in kind, in the flour from their own wheat and their own potatoes. He stood slightly dazed at the quantity of money, gold and silver, lying on the table in the lamplight. He took some of it and jingled it in his fingers. Finally he took half a sovereign and with a curious sensation of guilt and pleasure walked up into the streets of Nenweald and bought a doll for the child, a string of pink beads for Lily and a new Sunday hard hat for himself.

It was the year 1885. He felt extraordinarily elated. He had killed a fowl and had sent it, a peace offering, to his mother, and she, in return, had put down her pride and had been to see Lily and himself and the baby. He felt also a singular sense of peace and security. He wanted nothing finer or higher in life. If, as she expected, Lily was going to have another baby, all he asked was that it should be a son. He asked no more than that.

Lily alone was unsatisfied.

CHAPTER II

I

ONE winter afternoon, in the yard, he stood idle under the cart-hovel, watching a hare. Rain had been falling heavily all day. He could see the dark reflected clouds in the vast acres of flood-water extending far along the valley. The hare, light-coloured, almost golden against the rain-soaked earth, was running diagonally across the field in sudden starts of play and alarm, doubling and loping from side to side as it made for the lower hedge. He waited for it to disappear. Rain was still falling, in desultory spits that flecked and ringed the clay-coloured puddles about the yard. The hare was full-grown, a beauty. Then it struck him suddenly that it was the first he had noticed in the field. If he had ever seen another it had been unconsciously. And he stood transfixed in wonder.

When the hare had disappeared he found a length of wire and walked down the field, looping the wire as he went. The spot where the hare had vanished was clear in his mind. The land was sodden, the water squelching back everywhere into his footmarks. It was late January, his winter wheat was up and the young corn shoots lay flattened on the earth, like wet flags. As he went along under the hedge his shoulders brushed off drops of rain that hung on the reddish hawthorn twigs like beads of ice. And standing still he could see where the hare had capered across the wheat. Its little footprints had filled up, like his own, with yellowish water. And then he saw the gap. He went down on his knees to examine it. He could see by the broken brown skin of the split hawthorn twigs and the foot-padded earth that it was quite old. It had been in use a long time. Mystified, he thought: 'I ain't above half-alive. Damn, I must go about with me eyes shut.' He had scarcely to press back a twig or move a single grass in order to set his snare. It seemed too good to be true. And as he threaded the wire-loop and sharpened the ash-peg he felt a strange sense of excitement. He could hardly bear it. Something out of his past life came back to him, like a suddenly recollected emotion. His hands made the wire-loop almost unconsciously. He was like a swimmer cutting the water for the first time after a long absence. He sharpened the ash-peg carefully, and then slit it, very lightly, and then turned it round and round in his hands and looked at it. It was a beautiful peg. He had never made a better peg. Then he went down on his knees and looked at the gap again. He squinted through it like a man taking a gun-sight. Beyond the hedge the next field was pasture. By squinting through the run he could see across the grass the thin slightly padded tracks the hares had made by running to and fro. There were two tracks; and then he saw a third. They converged upon the gap like wheel-spokes. That meant that there were three at least and perhaps more hares passing regularly from one field to another. He stood up. He could scarcely believe it. He had been going about with his eyes shut. He had been so absorbed in the breaking up and planting of the field that he couldn't see what was under his own eyes. Christ, he was a born fool! He wiped the wire with his handkerchief and then, instinctively, without thinking, glanced round the field. There was not a soul in sight; nothing moving except the desultory rain and the boughs of the distant ash trees swinging flexibly up and down in the wind. He bent down and with his handkerchief gloved over his fingers set the snare. He moved with extreme lightness, scarcely touching the wire. And then, having finished it, he stepped back, at first two paces and then another. At the third pace the peg and the wire could no longer be distinguished from the twigs of hawthorn.

In the morning, coming down the field in the half-daylight, he found the hare, a buck, dead in the gap. There was no sign of a struggle, no blood, no torn fur. The wire had pulled up with extraordinary smoothness, like lightning, throttling the hare in a second. He felt a sense of almost fierce elation as he unwound the snare and put the wire in his pocket and went up the field with the hare in his hand.

He was so elated that he did something that morning he had never done before. Instead of eating his second breakfast in the hovel he went back home, just for the joy of showing Lily the hare. It was already nine o'clock when he returned, but Lily was still not up. He called upstairs. She answered sleepily. Then he lumbered upstairs, carrying the hare. When he reached the bedroom he held the hare behind his back, wanting to surprise her. Lily was lying half-asleep in the iron skeleton bed, with the child, Lizzie, still asleep beside her. He stood looking at them both, half-smiling, happy at the thought of surprising Lily, and all the time holding the hare behind his back. Lily was expecting a second baby in the spring and she was lying on her side, her eyes full of sleep, her hair in white curling-rags.

'What's the matter?' she said. 'What have you come back for?'

'I got summat for you.'

He whipped the hare from behind his back. A spot of the nose-blood, still not dry, flicked off and fell on the bed. Lily sat bolt upright in bed and shrieked.

'What is it? For God's sake, what *is* it?'

'What's a' matter?' he said, slowly. 'It's only a hare. That's all. What's a' matter?'

'Oh! it's awful, it's awful! Take it away, take it downstairs.'

Quite suddenly she began crying. The noise of her weeping and shouting woke the child, who sat up in bed and began crying too. He stood there bewildered. The hare hung down at his side. He did not know what to do. Lily looked strange and dowdy as she sat up in bed weeping, her curl-ragged hair falling about her face, which she had hidden in her hands. Finally he went towards the bed, ready to say something, and he had already stretched out his hand to touch her when she aroused herself and began shouting, her face white with the strain of her sudden rage.

She shouted for almost a minute before he began to understand the meaning of it all.

'It's only a hare,' he broke in once.

'Only a hare! Only a hare! That's all you think, that's all you trouble. How did you get it? You poached it, didn't you?'

'On me own land. I don't call that poaching.'

'You don't call it poaching! Then what is it? It isn't low-down cruelty, I suppose, is it? If you think you're going back to that game, you're much mistaken. I won't have it. I won't have Lizzie grow up to be the child of a poacher—you might as well know that now as later. I won't have it!' She had begun to wave her arms about with extreme excitement,

138

half-melodramatically. 'You don't want her to grow up ashamed of her father, do you?'

'No. But that ain't poaching.'

'I don't care what you call it! I know what I call it!' The child was crying more loudly than ever and suddenly Lily put her arms round her and hugged her close to her, as though she were in need of protection. The sound of Lily's shouts and the child's cries together grew into a mad confusion in Luke's mind, and he went off into a momentary stupor of bewilderment. Once or twice before it had seemed to him that she was living more and more apart from him, but the thought had never troubled him. But now he had a sudden suspicion, as she sat there in bed hugging Lizzie protectively to her, that she wanted to keep the child apart from him too.

A moment later she confirmed it by a shout of defiance:

'I want the child to grow up respectable, if you don't!'

It hurt him only when she suddenly ceased her shouting and turned to the child, lowering her voice and saying with softly bitter intimacy:

'We want you to grow up respectable, don't we? We want you to, don't we? Don't we?'

2

From that day he felt himself to be definitely in a world apart from Lily. He was forced more and more into himself and into the land. His solitary pleasure became the snaring of occasional hares. He kept it up secretly, selling the hares on the sly to old publican friends of his father's. Negotiations took him into Nenweald, but he had never time to linger in the place. He saw the growth of the town almost without realizing it, without seeing that it went along side by side with the growth of his little farm. Already the American river-digger had gone, the railway station had been built by the church, and there was talk of trams in the streets. He let it all go past him. It meant nothing to him; he had no comment on it. For him the atmosphere of the place remained the same as ever: the smell of the pubs under the whitewashed archways, the scent of the street limes in summer, the water-smell by the wharves where the barges came up laden with coal or grain or timber. He did not dream that it could change or that a change, if it came, could affect him. The same two strata of the town's society remained; he belonged to the lower and knew it and had no notion of rising any higher. The time he had spent on the land had, if anything, made him more uncouth. Eating alone, in ravenous snacks, among the pigs and hens, he behaved almost like an animal himself, smacking his lips, drinking his tea with a full mouth, with a sucking sound, wiping his knife across his mouth to lick off the gravy. It was these things that maddened Lily. 'How do you expect Lizzie to eat properly if you don't? Can't you eat without making people sick?' He would try drinking his tea silently or using his knife and fork in the proper manner, but the old habits would come back and Lily would give it up in a sort of savage despair.

He cared very little. Secretly, he centred all his hopes in the second child. A boy would put him on equal terms with Lily. Looking into the future, he saw himself teaching the boy to set a snare, to bait a line, to hold a scythe. They would work on the land together and then, at odd times, do a little poaching, on the quiet, just for amusement.

The second child was a girl. It was so like Lily that the triumph over him seemed to be complete, and he went back to work on the day of her birth with flat dejection. And instantly he began to see the future differently, making comfortless prophecies about it in his mind, thinking of how the two girls and Lily must grow up on one side and he, all alone, on the other.

And as though the bitterness of his disappointment had unconsciously given him the power of prophecy, the future began to turn out as he had half-imagined it. By 1890 the two little girls, Lizzie and Ellen, had become little dolls, with faces of white china and fair frizzy hair which crimped and rippled down their shoulders. In their stiff, thick-stuffed, many-pleated frocks they looked to him sometimes like little prim old women who would never grow any taller. They reminded him very often of his own two sisters: proud eyes, haughty noses, rather sleepy, languid lips. Lily spoke a correct rather clipped speech and in turn she taught it to the children. He had only to say 'God a'mighty, it's 'nation hot,' for her to fly into a rage: 'I won't have it! I won't *have* it! I'd rather they had their tongues cut out than let them talk like that. Don't you know any better?' He had no argument; it seemed to him the most natural speech in the world. It was Lily's correct clipped speech that was full of falsity. Yet he knew that he had no chance against it or her. '*I'll* bring the children up. At least they shall be brought up by someone who can read and write.' Sometimes a little of the old laconic irony would flash out in return. 'Ah, I dare say. Learn 'em to be ashamed o' their father and be done wi't.' But for the most part he was too tired to argue, or too resigned. Still, sometimes, he would try to reconcile the children. In the spring a stray pheasant or partridge would nest in his hedgerows or in the dead grass about the fruit trees and he would bring home a capful of eggs. 'Fry 'em for the gals.' But it was as though he had brought home snakes to be cooked. 'I *won't* have them. I've told you before about poaching.' He would say: 'It ain't poaching, on me own land. How do you make that out?' But she had only one argument. 'I won't *have* it. Yours or anyone else's land. I don't care. I won't *have* it.' So he would fry the eggs for himself, five or six at a time in the pan, taking them out as he needed them and wiping his bread in the pan when they were gone and then burning the shells. Even then Lily would not trust him.

'What did you do with those eggs?'

'Ah, I fried 'em all. Busted meself.'

'Busted? Busted? What language is that?'

And two years later, in 1892, Lily did what seemed to him a more extraordinary thing than she had ever done. The new Act for universal compulsory education had been passed, a new school had been built in Nenweald, and Lily, without warning, applied for a teacher's post. He knew nothing of it until his mother, who came to see him not more than once or twice a year, appeared one afternoon, half-running, half-walking across the field to where he was hoeing his barley. It was May, a hot moist day, and he could see the sweat standing on her forehead long before she reached him.

'What's a' matter?' he said.

'Make out you don't know!' she cried. 'Make out you don't know!'

'Know? Know what?' He stood leaning on his hoe, scratching his elbow and squinting his eyes against the strong sun.

And suddenly, in angry tones, she told him how it was all over the town that Lily had applied for the teacher's post and had been successful. 'All over the town!' she kept repeating. 'Everywhere.'

He stood in fixed meditation, trying to realize it.

'That's a licker!' he said at last. He could think of nothing else to say.

'A licker!' His mother was furious. Her black bonnet shook up and down with anger. For some reason she had brought an umbrella and she kept shaking that also. 'Ain't ye going to do anything about it?'

'What the 'nation can I do?'

'Ah, stick up for her,' she taunted him. 'Stick up for her.'

He could think of nothing to say or do either in answer to his mother or in reproval of Lily. He stood staring at the earth. There was a dock in the barley row and he bent down, clenched the leaves and pulled it up. He heard the sharp snap of the root breaking off, and suddenly he remembered the day he had broken off a dock at Thompson's farm and Thompson had kicked him in the back. It seemed a long time ago. He knew that at one time he would have smashed Thompson in the face, and he knew, similarly, that there had been a time when he would have been furious with Lily. But he was vaguely conscious that he had changed, that something had happened to him, that things which had been of importance were no longer of so much importance or were of no importance at all. He raised his eyes from the earth and looked across the field. The hedge was thick with new green leaves and half-opened creamy buds of May, so that he could see nothing beyond it. His world seemed to end there. He was not even sure that he wanted it ever to go beyond it. A curious contentment had come over him, a sluggishness in his blood, as though the soil had entered his veins.

And he discovered suddenly that he was not thinking of Lily, but only of the barley. He was admiring it. The young slender shoots, drilled in straight parallel lines with his new three-holed drill, looked beautiful in the sun. He had even forgotten his mother was standing there.

'Well, I got to git on wi' this barley,' he said.

'Ain't you going to do nothing about it?' she cried.

'She must do what she likes.'

'Going out to work!' she half-shouted. 'Your father would have knocked my head off! He'd have half-murdered me. A woman's place is in the house, and if she ain't sharp enough to know that, then be God I'll tell her!'

He had begun to hoe again, quietly, only half-listening to what she was saying, and finally she shouted:

'You're a blamed sight worse'n she is!'

'I dare say.'

She stood for a moment, antagonistically, before she turned and went away across the field. He turned once and looked at her and then went on.

3

Lily had realized some part of an ambition. The post of school teacher was a first step into a higher life. And being something new, a little daring, and against the conventions, it was also romantic. He saw this. And during the first few months of her school teaching he expected her at any moment to tire of it, to come home and say that she had given it up. But for some reason or other she kept on. And so the space between them widened and kept widening. But it was without pain, now, as though they were utterly hardened to it at last. He would be up before five in the morning, away to the field by six, and not back until darkness, which would be at four or five in the winter and never earlier than nine or ten in the summer. Lily and the two girls would be at school by nine each morning and back again by four in the afternoon. So that he saw them, sometimes, for no more than an hour or two a day, the girls sometimes not at all. They would be asleep when he returned from the field and either he would be too tired to go and look at them, or he would forget. Often he would come in, take off soil-dusty or muddy boots, throw them under the kitchen stove, sit in a chair to rest a moment, and drop off to sleep. There were times when he worked on, at harvest time, in the fine August moonlight, and when he sat up all night with a farrowing sow. He was fond of his pigs. He kept them zealously, raised litters, chose the best for breeding or killing and marketed the rest. He bought a large barrel and for a time kept it outside the back door of the house, so that neighbours could empty into it all sorts of refuse, cabbage stalks, bread, potato peel, rotted fruit, for his pig swill. Then Lily protested: 'It's disgusting, filthy. I want to be sick whenever I *look* at it!' So he removed it, getting the garbage by taking the barrel from house to house on his flat cart and making a collection like a scavenger. That made Lily more furious still, so furious that, meeting him trundling about the streets with the barrel, she would disown him. And then he noticed that the children began to use the front door, an unheard-of innovation. Only the select, moneyed, leisured classes used the front door. It was sacred. He knew of front doors that had remained shut for so long that they had stuck or jammed and could never, except by force, be opened again. He, like all workers, came in at the back, wiping his boots on the door-sack. And the use of different doors seemed to set them farther apart still. The two doors in actuality led into different streets, and the streets seemed to lead into different worlds.

And in his world, so very small, bounded by the four hawthorn hedges of the field, he lived simply and a bit crudely, in communion with himself and the land and the few animals he had. He ceased after a time to trouble much about ambition. Then, by the end of the century, he ceased to trouble about it at all. He began to do the same things year in, year out. He exhausted all the variations of crop rotation. He fell into a rut. Now and then he suffered a catastrophe: swine-fever devastated his pigs, a thunderstorm laid his wheat beyond recovery, a fox broke in and slaughtered his hens, but somehow, at the end of each year, he seemed to stand where he had stood at the end of the last. There was never a time when he could not pay his rent. But similarly there was never a time when he could rent another acre or two of land, or buy another horse or hire another man. He never took a holiday. He felt that he had some sort of duty to his pigs and hens and he would never leave them. So he became more and more solitary, bound up in himself, always working alone, sometimes not speaking to another soul during the whole day, but only talking to himself in a half-conscious mutter of comfort or rebuke or introspection as he worked backwards and forwards across the unchanging field.

But though the field seemed to remain the same he himself, in appearance more noticeably, began to change. As a youth, and beside his father especially, he had been extremely thin, almost spidery, walking with a perpetual slouch and swagger, his face sallow and almost fleshless. The perpetual work on the land thickened him so that, though he was never fat, he began to have a solid and muscular appearance. He was more like his father. His arms were like stocky clubs made up of many knots and twists of whipcord, the colour of some coppery-red cow. His face was like an Indian's, though altogether milder, with no fierceness at all, his eyes a sky-grey, distant and full of a meditative quietness.

But strangely, though he was thicker and more powerful, he seemed to be smaller. He was not so tall by an inch or two. He walked with a slight stoop, his head sunk. It was at first a stoop of necessity. He stooped to hoe or to hold the plough handles or to swing his scythe or to plant his potatoes. Then it became habitual. He stooped wherever he went, whatever he was doing, without ever being aware of it except when Lily, infuriated, drew his attention to it:

'Hold yourself up! You're beginning to stoop like an old man. Hold yourself straight.'

She herself, like the girls, had a rigid, broad-backed figure, corseted into contemporary shape by tremendous whale-bone stays which, when he saw them lying about in the bedroom, made him wonder how she ever moved or breathed. She cultivated a style of hairdressing, piling the hair into a high cone, which made her seem even straighter and taller than she was. Then when neck-frills, bone-sided, became fashionable, she wore those also, so that sometimes, towards the end of the century, he would think of her as a stick dressed up. And the years of school-teaching had already left their mark on her as plainly as the land had left its mark on him. She spoke and acted in a frigid, domineering way, her speech rapped out in command or reprimand, her voice high-pitched. But like him she was unaware of the changes in herself. And though he saw them he said nothing, just as he said nothing when she invited other school teachers or ladies of the town to tea in the front parlour and set out his own cup and plate in the kitchen at the back. He would eat in comfort alone. 'Dalled if the grub tastes the same,' he would think, 'among a 'nation lot o' females.'

But she still remained, in a fitful way, not only ambitious for herself and the girls, but for him too. There was scarcely a social, a conversazione, a meat tea, a jubilee celebration to which she did not ask him to go if she were invited. And sometimes, dressed in his Sunday black, with squeaky calf boots which he wore no more than five or six times a year, he would go with her, the husband of Mrs. Bishop, the schoolmistress.

He behaved tolerably enough until he sucked his tea through his moustache like a pig at trough or remarked 'Plenty o' grub, missus. Regular slap-up. Let's have another mossel o' that kid's pap,' meaning the trifle. Then there would be fury, high-sounding disgust and recriminations when they got home.

'Why did you go and pour your tea in your saucer?'

'Damn, it wor' hot.'

'Hot! You couldn't let it cool, I suppose! Oh no.'

'I bin harrowing all day. I wor ready for that cup o' tea.'

'Ready! I should think so. Scoffing it like a pig.'

'I wasn't the only one as saucered. I see one or two chaps—'

'Two blacks don't make a white. It made me sick!'

But after a time she seemed to forget it, her ambition for him renewed itself, and she would try again. It was as though, deep within her, she retained a scrap of imperishable gratitude towards him for taking her away from Thompson and the stiff intolerable life of the farm. She had sense enough to see that but for him she would never have been where she was. And in a sense, except for his lapses of taste and behaviour, she was happy where she was. She had gained for herself a sort of independence, based at first on a harmless notoriety and then on complete respectability. And the two girls, who were already probationary teachers too, seemed to consolidate that happiness.

And then, at the very end of the century, when there was nothing but talk of change and hope and the glorious future and the new age, something happened to make her happier still.

The headmistress of the school died, the post was thrown vacant, and Lily succeeded to it.

Luke stood amazed, dazzled by the event, and in a vague way a little proud of Lily.

'Damn,' he said, 'you're notch above a tapper now.'

'Don't use such talk!' she said. 'Common expressions! I'd be *above* them.'

'Well,' he said, 'it's right. You're top o' the tree.'

'Well, I suppose I am.'

'Means some more dough, I warrant.'

'There you go again. Dough! Isn't it just as easy to say money?'

'Money, then.'

'Well, it does. A little. But I need it. I want to give the girls a good start in life. I want to see them get on.'

And at the end of the year, which was also the end of the century, there were all the ribald, illuminated, shouting celebrations. The school held its special celebration, welcoming not only the new century, but the new headmistress: a meat tea, fireworks to follow, banners and flags on the school belfry, the playground lit up with gaslight. It was a kind of minor coronation for Lily, with the two girls, like two princesses, strengthening the effect.

At the last moment Luke, with a sow in farrow, found it difficult to go. He could only promise to try and drop in for the midnight celebrations, and only that if the sow were to deliver easily or quickly. So that, instead of going to the celebrations, he sat with the pig in the lantern-lit sty, on the new fragrant straw he had put down for her. And now and then he would leave the sty and go outside and stand in the outside darkness, and look and listen. The sky above the town was filled with a soft arc of reflected light. He could see the church spire. The night was very still, the fields all about him full of the black silence of winter, and now and then he could hear the faint noises of celebration, bugle-calls, the playing of the brass band, the crack of fireworks. And the sky, sometimes, would be split by a rocket bursting into sparks of crimson and blue and emerald that vanished more quickly than falling stars.

PART FOUR: THE NEW CENTURY

CHAPTER I

I

AT the beginning of the new century Nenweald was still a little town. It had all the littleness of self-satisfied content. The railway had come, warehouses had begun to be built beside it, and in the back streets more and more factories had begun to spring up, flat-faced three-storied buildings sandwiched in between the rows of flat-faced two-storied houses. New streets of red brick were being built to the very edges of the green fields, and here and there clubs and temperance halls and chapels, all of the same red brick, were rising up among the little shops of the fashionless country tailors and drapers who changed their fly-specked windows once a week but in reality never changed them at all. Nothing was being changed; only something was being added. The heart of the place, exemplified by the little chestnut-shaded Square lying close under the big church, remained fixed as though unalterable, its little change a mere cycle of ritual, like the thickening and dying and falling of the chestnut leaves and chestnut blossoms. Old men sleeping and dozing on summer afternoons in the chestnut shade were never disturbed except by the passing of a chance threshing-machine or an engine steaming to a fair. And the men in green livery or sun-faded black and ageless top-hats waiting at the station with their cabs and landaus for the arrival of the trains could doze in peace too, since the trains were few and the passengers needing conveyances fewer still. On those summer afternoons the streets would be heavy with the scent of street limes and the warm odour of horse-dung mingled together, only the sudden acrid stink of leather and wax from some hot factory disturbing or overpowering it, the odour as prevalent as incense and as full of sleepiness as the warm water-smell in the low-lying meadows at the river-side. They were scents and odours which were as much a part of the place as the white-aproned shoemakers fetching their Sunday dinners of batter-pudding from the back-street bakehouses, or as the little backyard shoemaking shops had been twenty and even ten years before.

For if nothing was changing or seeming to change in the place itself there was a change in the shoemakers. With the springing up of the factories the little individual shops were dead or doomed. The shoemakers were caught up in an iron system of time; their independence began to perish. There were School Acts and Factory Acts. The little sweaters, boys the shoemakers had employed to run eternal errands and wax eternal string with eternal sweat, were caught up by the School Acts, the men were caught up by the Factory Acts, and gone in a minute were the half-days to watch a circus procession, the whole days to follow the fox-hounds, the sobering-up Mondays, the odd hours off for political arguments or fights to settle what Bradlaugh said, and finally and most of all the long weeks taken off in the late summer for the harvest. The flame of that shifting and independent life was suddenly snuffed out. And in its place came an artificial, fixed, incandescent gas-flame kind of life, a life that burned for a given period and was turned off. It burned behind the thick glass factory windows just as a gas burns behind the mantle-globe, protected, shut away. Then, when it was turned off, for the dinner-hour or the evening, some of the old life flamed up again. At noon the streets were thronged, the street-corner fights were renewed, the factories stood silent. Until suddenly the time-whistles or buzzers blew, there was a brief white fluttering of vanishing aprons, and the afternoon silence descended, a silence broken only by the regulated moan and murmur of the machines, a curious imprisoned, mournful sound, stifled, that never penetrated the unaltered somnolence of the Square under the shadow of the chestnut trees.

Up in the field, alone, Luke scarcely noticed the first additions and changes in the life of the town below. Days melted into each other and weeks and years into each other, without a perceptible difference, just as one century had melted into another. Time travelled past him like a wind. He had no friends. In the early poaching days his father had discountenanced the making of friendships. 'We don't trust nobody. Why should we? Nobody trusts us.' The whole of that early life had been filled with secrecy and a suspicion for other people that Luke had never outlived. In the new century there was no one to whom he could turn for advice or help except his aunt, who still lived on, very old and little by little growing more toothless and more sardonic and more difficult. She had begun to cut herself off from the world, leaving notes on the doorsteps for the tradesmen, never answering knocks and seeing no one but him. The decay and ache preceding the fall of each tooth brought on alternate periods of savagery and gloom. She would sit with her face bound up with a vast red silk handkerchief, the brandy bottle at her side, her lower lip in a perpetual pout, lumps of brandy-soaked cotton-wool and matchsticks ready on the table beside her. Now and then she would renew the cotton-wool in the tooth, take a sip of brandy to fortify herself, growl in fresh wretchedness. The handkerchief bound up over her ears made her a little deaf, so that Luke, sitting on the other side of the fireplace, was obliged to get up every time he spoke, funnel his hands over his mouth, and shout.

'Have it out,' he would say. 'Be done with it.'

'Eh?'

'Have it out! Go and see Maudlin. He'll nip it out afore you can wink.'

'Um. What about those mushrooms?'

'What mushrooms? I was talking about your tooth.' He would get up, go over to her and shout into her ear. 'Your tooth!'

'I can hear, I can hear.'

'All right. Your tooth, why don't you have it out?'

'That's what I say. You promise things and then don't do 'em. How's Lily?'

'All right.'

'She never comes to see me.'

And then a twinge of pain, and then more cotton-wool and more brandy; and after that a renewal of her reproaches and deafness and his own shouting.

So that sometimes, when he had a problem to face or a decision to make and would have otherwise discussed it with her, he would let it pass and did not trouble her. In this way there were certain things which he let slide. He kept intending to do things and never did them. It occurred to him that instead of renting his field he might buy it, and he intended to discuss that with her and never did.

And so with his horse. Ever since the first years of the little farm he had kept a horse, generally a rough light cart-horse which he could use both for the plough and for the trap in which he sometimes drove Lily about the country-side on summer evenings. Periodically, as a horse grew old and as he saw the chance of a bargain, he would change one horse for another. And there grew up a series of unspoken friendships, so that he got to know a horse intimately and hated to part with it.

Then, as he was driving out of Nenweald one August morning, wondering if his oats would soon be ready, his horse, a pure white, suddenly slipped, the cart lurched askew across the road and the horse was down. Staggering out of the cart, he saw a sudden gush of blood on the white horsehair where the shaft had punctured the flank. And almost before he could realize it the knacker's cart was there, he heard the dull flat report of the horse-pistol and the dead horse was being loaded and driven away.

His oats were almost ready, harvest was coming on. In desperation, a bit stupefied, he took the train next day to Orcester and bought another horse, a light brown mare, from a dealer there. When he arrived back at the field in the late afternoon a stranger was sitting under the haystack in the yard, waiting for him. He wore a bowler hat and carried a leather case with him.

'I represent the Eastern Counties Accident and Life Insurance Company. I hear you've lost a horse,' he said rapidly.

'Ah.'

'Was it insured?'

'No.'

'Not insured! There you are! Now I represent the Eastern Counties Accident and Life Insurance Company and we insure—'

They talked together for a long time in the yard, first standing by the stack and then walking backwards and forwards as Luke mixed the pig-swill and went to and fro with the buckets, the insurance agent jabbering and following him wherever he went, Luke promising nothing but 'I ain't got the new horse yet. I'll think it over. I'll see at th' end o' the week.'

The next day the insurance agent arrived again and went on with the rigmarole like one of the talking-machines just then coming into popularity. 'We insure against accident, or disease, or fire, or lameness. Or if your horse goes sick—'

'I never had horse go sick yet.'

'Well, there's a first time to everything.'

'I'll think it over. I'll see th' end o' the week.'

'Think it over now. I'll wait.'

'I ain't got time. I want to git my oats knocked down.'

Three mornings later, as he went down the hedge-side to catch the mare, he could see from a distance that she was lying in the long ditch-grass. She seemed to be in a strange attitude, with her neck stretched out. Hurrying down, he found that she had noosed her head in a fence gap, much as a rabbit would in a snare, and that as she had pulled it out again a bare fence-nail had ripped her neck. She was already half-dead when he reached her. By the time he had run up to the stable and back again with a sack to staunch the blood-flow there was nothing else he could do but give a message to a passing carter and then wait for the knacker to come.

He went about for the rest of the day with a feeling of bitterest anger, the only real bitterness he had felt since Thompson had kicked him. And he felt it against himself, for his own foolishness. By evening he felt exhausted by it. It seemed to go round and round inside him, as though it could find no outlet.

Going home, he sat down in the kitchen and took off his dust-powdered boots and put them under the stove. He sat quietly for a minute or two with his sweat-tired feet on the cool bricks, resting, feeling a little better.

And then he thought he could hear someone crying. The sound seemed to come from the front parlour. He listened. The dismal fretting sound was unmistakable. And then he could hear also a voice talking, upraised for a moment, and then lowered, in a crescendo of earnest insistence. It seemed like Lily's voice, and after listening for another moment or two he got up and went into the front parlour.

He was still in his stockinged feet, he walked silently, and Lily and Lizzie were startled when he opened the door. And for a moment the crying and the talking ceased.

He stood with his hand on the door-knob, confused, not knowing what to say. Neither Lily nor Lizzie spoke to him. He could see that Lizzie had been crying. She was sitting on a horsehair sofa, with her handkerchief round her fingers. Lily was standing up.

They stood like that for a moment or two, not speaking, he staring at them but neither of them looking at him, until at last he asked what was the matter. It did not occur to him until he had asked the same thing a second time that they might have heard about the mare. But it was too late then. Lily, looking at Lizzie, was saying:

'I think she had better tell you herself.'

Lizzie shook her head.

'I think so,' said Lily.

Something in Lily's voice, a little hard and ironically aloof, reminded him of Thompson. And he felt a sudden flood of sympathy for the girl sitting there with the tears beginning to run quietly down her face again.

'Come, come, my gal,' he said, 'what's a' matter?'

Lizzie shook her head again, so that the falling tears were shaken off her face.

'Trouble anew,' he said, 'without you tunin'. What's a matter, my gal?'

He spoke quietly, the anger and bitterness about the dead mare dissolved by his sympathy for her. But the girl did not speak and finally Lily said:

'Am I to tell him?' And then began before the girl could answer: 'If he had any eyes of course he could see for himself.'

The girl began suddenly to cry afresh, loudly, with her head on her knees, in inarticulate despair.

'No use crying,' said Lily, and the voice again reminded him of Thompson. 'Crying won't help it. What's done is done.'

Then he saw the cause of it all. And suddenly he felt a return of all the anger he had experienced during the day. And it returned not against himself or the horse but against Lily. He found himself suddenly raising his voice:

'Why the 'nation don't you leave the gal alone?'

Lily stared at him. 'Do you know what *is* the matter?' she said. She spoke in a voice that was horrified. 'Do you know she's going to have a baby?'

'God a'mighty, what if she is?' he shouted.

'You don't know what you're saying!' she said.

'Shut up!' he shouted.

Astounded, not knowing what to say, she let him walk past her without another word to where Lizzie was crying on the sofa. And he, as he stood over the girl telling her not to cry, to dry her eyes and to come to her senses, felt suddenly a flood of quiet tenderness amounting almost to relief.

'Come, come, God a'mighty, it's nothing. Anybody'd think you'd lost a sovereign and found a farden. You ain't the first. Not in this family either. As long as you know who it is, it don't matter a sight.'

'That's what I've been trying to get at from her all the evening,' Lily said. 'But she will not tell me.'

'She'll tell me. Come, come now. Dry your eyes. You know who 'tis, don't you?'

'Yes.'

'Well, who is it?'

'He's all right. He'll marry me.'

'All right. What's his name?'

'Walter Vine.' She was beginning to cry again. 'He's all right. He's a foreman.'

'Who for?'

'Joyce's. It's a good job.'

'All right. Dry your eyes. That's all right. You'd better bring this Walter in to see your mother.'

She was crying again, in a sudden burst of relief, as he suddenly turned and walked out of the room, feeling almost ridiculous in his soundless stockinged feet. It was not until he reached the kitchen and was drawing the water to wash himself that he remembered that he had said nothing to Lily about the mare. He was too tired to go back into the parlour to tell her then and it was not until the following evening that he said anything about it to her at all. By that time she had heard of it from someone else and he had hired another horse.

3

Walter became one of the family. He was a tallish, fair-haired young man with extremely fresh blue eyes and a light brown moustache of which he was very proud. He wore good serge suits and on Sundays a straw-hat or a bowler. He was a regular chapel-goer and sang in the choir, and when he and Lizzie had been married and were settled in the front parlour Luke would hear Walter practising his rich bass

voice in the evenings, accompanying himself rather solidly
on the piano he had brought to the house with him. He had
no parents, had lived in lodgings, and was elated by the idea
of marriage and a home. And from the very first Luke liked
him; they got on well together. Surrounded since the death
of his father by women, Luke felt an extraordinary sense of
pleasure in the thought of constant male companionship.
Walter was a man of rational, logical views, Luke in a sense
was a mild revolutionary, and in the evenings after harvest
they would have long argumentative talks, oblivious of time,
so that finally Lizzie or Lily would need to call them to bed.
Luke felt invigorated and refreshed. With a lodger in the
house and the argumentative atmosphere it seemed to him
like old times. And Walter brought him another stimulus.
On Saturday afternoons and sometimes in the evenings
Walter put on old clothes and came to help in the field. He
had a genius for construction. He adored to pull things down
and build them afresh. And the ramshackle cart-hovels and
stables and hen-houses, built by Luke nearly twenty years
before and patched up ever since by bits of rusted tin or
corrugated iron, appalled him. They would have to be re-
built. Things would have to be put on a proper basis. Walter
was amazed that anything had survived, that Luke had
escaped bankruptcy; and he would walk about the stack-
yard in silence, ruminating, taking mental measurements,
squinting his eyes, constructing it all afresh in his mind.
'You're behind the times, all behind,' he would say. 'Things
are altering. You must catch up.' And he would go about
knocking on pieces of dung-rotted wood or patches of tin
rusted by time and weather almost to powder. 'It's rotten,' he
would say. 'The whole place is rotten.' Then he arranged for
surplus packing-cases to be sent up to the field from the
factory for which he worked, and then he would hear of
cheap bricks or cheap wholesale lots of corrugated iron, and
Luke would fetch them in the cart. And there he would be,
every Saturday, sawing and hammering with immense
energy between long intervals of almost sombre constructive

thought, until gradually the place began to change. Fresh white wooden buildings with shiny grey iron roofs and brick foundations sprang up instead of the ramshackle bramble-roofed hovels. Walter fitted cunning patent trap-doors to the hen-coops and proper drainage in the pig-sties, the stable was reconstructed, and then an entirely new cow-house made. A cow was an ambition Luke had never realized. 'Call yourself a farmer and not keep a cow!' Walter would saw and hammer away in disgust. 'You must have a cow.' So they built a cow-house, with room enough for six cows. 'You want room to extend,' Walter said. By the time the cow-house was finished it was winter. So Walter turned to the fruit-trees, pruning them with religious care on cold fine winter after-noons, so that they stood sparse and shapely against the sky. Then, when it was all finished and the wet and cold and the short days of winter made new work impossible, Walter would come to the field for the mere pleasure of walking about, sizing up his handiwork and creating in his mind fresh worlds for summer and spring. He was very proud, solidly, decently proud of his work. But like Lily he was never satisfied. He built new worlds on the roofs of the old almost before the foundations of the old were finished. He hated to go back. He had to turn his back on the past and go forward. And it plunged him into despondency and almost broke his heart when a fox raided the reconstructed hen-house, bur-rowed under the new wooden walls and took off half the hens. It was not the loss of the hens that humiliated him, but the thought of going back into the past that hurt him. And he set to work to build a brick fox-proof barricade, two feet high, round the hen-house, so that it should never occur again.

In Walter, Luke saw the whole changing world of the new century personified. 'No flies on Walter,' he would think. Walter would get on. He had the fervour and ambition not only of youth but of youth fed on a new diet of education. Walter had no use for the old, physical, swaggering, drunken, brawling mode of life, glamorous but wasteful, the life that the youth of Luke's own day had lived. He worked hard and regularly, never drank, saved his money, put in three evenings a week at the new night school, read Darwin and Dickens, and then still had time to teach himself the theory of music. Above all he had his own genius for construction, for planning what he would do with the future, not content to let the future drift towards him and carry him where it would. And the things he planned to do were successful. 'On'y got to think on it, Walt has, and it's done,' Luke would say. 'Masterpiece!'

In every way the coming of Walter was like an injection of new life. Luke felt a sense of splendid rejuvenation. That winter Walter began to subscribe to a weekly paper for smallholders in addition to the newspaper he already took in every morning. In it were articles on the scientific manuring of soil, the breeding of pigs, machinery, poultry on up-to-date lines, marketing and distribution, rabbit-keeping for profit, everything, all accompanied by explanatory line-drawings of men drawing rule-straight drills and furrows and growing perfect crops on perfect land. Luke and Walter read and studied it together. Luke regarded it with the suspicion of experience, but to Walter it was the stern pattern of perfection on which Luke had to begin to remodel all his ways. Things had to be different. The old shifty, careless ways had to go. Luke must keep accounts, put his money in the bank, have an eye to business. And sitting over the agricultural paper they would plan great things together for the spring, a real renaissance, a new glory.

It was a renaissance that seemed of no importance at all when spring did come and Lizzie had a son.

CHAPTER II

I

THE birth of a grandson was a miracle. It put about Luke's head a kind of halo of absurd happiness and light. It forced him at once to live a life other than his own, the boy's life. It filled him with an anxiety to live not as he had always done, in the present and the past, but more as Lily and Walter did, in the future. He at once looked forward with eagerness to the day when the boy would grow up. He began to shape his childhood and even his manhood for him. The boy featured Walter, was very fair, slim and lively, with extremely light blue eyes. Stroking his very soft hair or touching his even softer skin Luke would say: 'A little leveret. Damn, he's like a little leveret.' Or 'Look at the size of that head. That ain't no ordinary head. He's going to be a notch above Walt, you can see that.' And all day, on the land, he would go about thinking of him, watching the road also on the chance that Lizzie might be wheeling him out in his boat-shaped yellow wicker perambulator, wretched if she did not come, full of a kind of silly tender delight if she did. Then in the summer the boy was christened. There was the problem of his name Lizzie would have him called Walter; but Walter objected. 'It'll be Big Walter and Little Walter,' he said. 'That'll mix us up.' He would have John. But hearing it, Luke recited:

'Matthew, Mark, Luke and John,
Hold my horse while I get on,
If he . . .'

and that was the end of it. Then Lily suggested Edward. 'After the King,' she said. About that time a big new chapel of red brick and slate had been built in the High Street, with straight-backed, comfortless pitch-pine seats, a gallery, and many brass gas chandeliers and coloured windows, a symbol of high respectability and the town's progress. And finally the child, Edward, was the first to be christened in it and Lizzie and Walter were presented with a Bible inscribed to commemorate the occasion. It was as though the child had been dedicated to the church and the throne. And Lizzie and Walter foresaw for him a life of extreme uprightness, godliness and ultimate success, with a position perhaps in one of the new banks springing up among the new shops and offices along the High Street. A new town was being made and Edward would grow up with it. The old stone houses were being pulled down and shops of new red brick replacing them, and it was a good thing. Just as it was a good thing that the traffic of barges was ceasing along the river and that there would be no more bargees invading the town on Saturday evenings, brawling in the pubs, and heckling the Salvation Army, as it worshipped on the Square. It seemed to Lizzie and Walter that the entire remodelling of the town's life was needed. So much that was crude and coarse must be swept away. It was the age of tight waists and even tighter rules of conduct, and Lizzie and Walter went to chapel twice on Sunday and sometimes to a prayer-meeting during the week, believing very much in the efficacy of prayer and the respectability of holiness. Once, after hearing almost with tears a sermon on the evils of gambling, Walter hurried home, seized a box of dominoes and threw them on the fire. And the child, as soon as he could walk, was taken to the chapel and the Sunday school. Lizzie dressed him very early in little blue serge suits and in sailor-suits of blue and white and a blue sailor's cap with the name of the ship in white letters round the brim. He would sit in the choir with his father, invisible, staring at the pink angels in the stained-glass windows or at the crotchets and quavers in the tune-book that his father gave him to keep him quiet during the sermon and the prayers. And as he began to grow up he could feel the strange Sunday silence hanging over the town, over the fields, over the whole world, as though it were a sin to move or speak except behind the chapel doors and the pink-angeled windows.

So on Sundays he seemed to belong wholly to his father and mother, to be part of their life, the life of respectability and singing and silence. But during the week he belonged to Luke. From the very first they began to grow up in perfect understanding. In the long days before he began at school the boy would be in the field all day. He began very early to behave with imitative manfulness, spitting like his grandfather, switching his legs with an ash-stick, scratching the sows' backs, holloaing at the horse or the hens. On the scorching hot days of harvest Luke would put him to sleep in the shade of a wheat-shock; on wet days they would sit under the hovel or in the stable. They would sit watching the continuous western rain falling softly over the dark land, nothing disturbing the monotony of its fall except the sleepy chucking of the cooped-up hens, and Luke's voice unwinding like a tangled wool-skein some story of him and his father poaching, running from the police or fighting with the keepers, the story itself broken only by the boy's eternal questions.

'Why'd you do it in the dark? At nights?'

'Safest. Get pulled too easy in daylight.'

'What's pulled?'

'Pulled? You know that. Collared. Clap you in quod afore you can wink.'

'Did you ever get pulled?'

'Near as nick it. Times.'

'And in quod?'

'No. Had some near squeaks. But they never got me. Same with th' old Dad. We were too fly for 'em.'

'What's fly?'

'Fly. You know that. God a'mighty, you're fly enough yourself. . . .'

And then the tale would be renewed, the questions would break it again, and so on, until the ceasing of the rain would end it all. Then, in season, Luke would set a snare or two and the boy would go along the hedge-sides with him.

'You keep your eyes open while I'm a-bending down. See anybody?'

'No. Yes! Man on a bike.'

'Ain't looking?'

'No. It's all right. He's gone.'

And the boy would stand under the hedge in tense silence, listening and watching, his heart thundering, while Luke set the snare.

'Anybody about?'

'No.'

'All right.' And then always the last warning, secretive, and intensely serious:

'Know what I told you? You don't let on to your Dad about this?'

'No.'

'Never?'

'No.'

'All right. Don't you never let on. Never. D'ye understand that? Never.'

It was a warning he spoke with almost desperate earnestness, knowing perfectly the consequences of its being disobeyed. He saw clearly the chances of the boy being snatched away from him, how easily the new, respectable school-and-chapel life would claim him. And sometimes, as they sat in the cart-hovel, he would catechize the boy.

'What do they learn you at Sunday school, eh? Jesus and all that?'

'And Moses. A lot about Moses.'

'Striking the rock and gettin' the water out? That tale?'

'It's a miracle.'

'Miracle? Who said so? You don't believe he got that water out, all of a pop, like that? It's only a tale, made up. Don't ye know that? It's only a lot o' popery.'

The boy would consider this. It was impressive. Moses would wage against his grandfather in his mind.

'What else do they tell you? About the bulrushes? That tale?'

'Yes. About the baby.'

'That's a good tale.'

'It's true, though.'

'It ain't true! It's popery. See that? Made up. God a'mighty. Bulrushes! Ah, come on, let's get on and cut them cabbages.'

All the time Walter and Lizzie were saving money so that the boy might go away to school. Lizzie, like Lily, kept on teaching. Walter worked hard and soberly at the factory. So that the boy, in a sense, led two lives, absorbing them

163

both, not differentiating between them, stealing pheasants'
eggs as easily as he said his prayers and learning to set a snare
as quickly as he learned the Creed. He was growing up
gentle, quick-witted, rather like Walter, with a passionate
energy for doing things, for going forward. It seemed already
that he would get on in life, do great things, be somebody. At
times, in the evenings, he would sit on a stool by the fire and
read aloud to Luke from the newspaper, stuttering out the
longest words, mastering the political news as easily as the
trivialities and the gossip.

'Read that bit again. No fixed abode.'

'James Church, drover, no fixed abode, was to-day
summoned at Orcester.'

'Thought I knowed him. Drunk?'

'Drunk and disorderly at Orcester market on Wednesday
last, and for using obscene language towards—'

'That's it. That's him. Never could hold his beer.'

'Defendant was fined ten shillings or one month.'

'Take the month?'

'Yes. Defendant—'

'That's the boy, I knowed 'im. I recollect the time—'

And the newspaper would give way to reminiscence, the
reminiscence resolving itself into a story, the story winding
on and on with everlasting fascination, unbroken until Lily
or Lizzie or even Walter came in and brought it abruptly to
an end:

'Give over, Father; give over, do. Filling the boy's head
with nonsense, silly tales. Give over.'

They had begun to call him Father. It was more respectable, more high-sounding, a little impersonal. It was an
indication of the changes that were coming over the house as
well as over the town. He could see or sense endless changes
everywhere. No one but himself now washed at the sink in the
kitchen, or sat by the fire and took off their boots and set
them to dry, sideways, by the stove. The rest of the family
washed upstairs. Only he splashed and spluttered at the sink,
naked to the waist, his breeches held up by his twisted

braces. And he sensed, vaguely, that he was becoming an outsider, different, a bit common. For years he had never felt close to Lily, and now, as years went by, he began to feel more distant than ever. Blouses were coming into fashion, and Lily wore one of a striped shirt pattern, with the close masculine collar brooched at the neck, her relentless corsets stiffening and repressing her bust to an iron shape, so that at fifty she had a look of extreme, almost military uprightness and severity. She smelt of camphor. And he could see her, in imagination, addressing the children of her school as sometimes she addressed Eddie and even himself in the home: '*Eddie! Luke! Will* you *learn* to *behave* yourselves?' And then he would try to disentangle from the past an image of her as he had first known her, very long ago, on the Thompson's farm. But he could never do it. It was as though he had seen her in a dream: as though time had worked some curious trick of metamorphosis on her. Then he would think that perhaps it wasn't Lily who had changed or was different, but himself. He was an old toad, a fool. An easy-going old fub. No good. Where had he got in thirty years? Nowhere. He was nobody. They were all getting on, farther and higher in the world, except him. It was only the boy, and the constant thought and hope for him, and in return the boy's worship of himself, that saved him from the completest self-negation and despair.

There were times also when he suspected that Lily, the two girls and Walter were together in some kind of conspiracy against him. Walter rarely came up to the field. All his work there was a thing of the past. He was advancing towards something else, conceiving new ideas. He had been promoted to choir-master at the chapel, was studying music zealously, and had taken some shares in the partnership of the boot factory. He was talked about, respected, a little envied. When neighbours were troubled by some intricate form that had to be filled up they came to Walter, and Walter signed the form, straightened things out, gave them advice. He had no longer any time for the old evening arguments with Luke, the warm discussions of his early married life. His time was wholly occupied. But he was still likeable, full of life, friendly. It was only that he was living more and more apart, in the new life of chapels and town-progress and business. Once or twice Luke expected that Walter and Lizzie would move, with the boy, to a house of their own, one of the many new bay-windowed houses that were already eating up the green fields. But living altogether with Luke and Lily made it possible for Lizzie to go on teaching while Emma did the housework, and Lizzie and Walter could go on saving money for the boy's education. So they remained, waiting with a kind of tender, blind patience for the day when the boy would be able to go away, Luke dreading the approach of the time even more than they ever hoped for it.

And sometimes it was as though the whole family half-suspected that he would one day upset all their plans, so carefully and beautifully laid, for their own and the boy's progress. He could think of no other reason for the conspiracy they seemed to hold against him.

Then as he sat in the kitchen, one evening, pulling off his boots, Lizzie came in and went out again quickly without speaking. A moment later he could hear her voice in the front parlour. The doors stood open, her voice was not lowered, and he could hear Lily's plainly in answer.

'He smells,' Lizzie said. 'Go and say something to him.'

'Aren't I for everlasting saying something to him?'

'He's been cleaning pigs or something.'

'I've spoken to him until I'm tired of speaking.'

'It's disgusting. One can *taste* it.'

Then Lizzie came back. He was standing at the sink, in his stockinged feet, preparing to wash. Lizzie came in and said:

'Father, put your boots outside.'

'Ah, they won' hurt, my gal.'

'Father, do as I say.'

'What's a' matter wi' em?'

'You know what's the matter. Put them outside.'

'Ah, stink a bit, do they? It's only a mossel o' pig muck. I bin cleaning out.'

'Then you'd better give up keeping pigs.'

'Give up keeping—'

'Yes, and another thing. Get yourself a shave. You look like a tramp.'

'It's on'y Tuesday,' he said. 'Shaving night's a' Wednesday.'

'Well, get one *now* for a change!'

'But shaving night's a' Wednesday,' he said.

'I don't care if it is!' Suddenly she began to shout. 'If you can't come home a little decent you must be made to! I've stood it long enough. You live among pigs and things until you're nothing better than a pig yourself!'

'Ah!' It was a return of the old ironical, casual half-bitter tone of his youth. 'And I'm ye Dad, too, ain't I?'

'That's no reason why you should make me ashamed of you, is it?' she shouted.

She suddenly lifted the boots off the stove, opened the door and flung them into the yard outside, and then vanished into the parlour without another word.

He stood staring out of the window, his hands feeling for the water in the wash-bowl, his mind dead. It was the first time they had shown him openly that they wanted to be rid of him.

And then, not long afterwards, he came home one evening to find Lily and the two girls and Walter sitting silent round the living-room, staring at each other solemnly, as though at a meeting of some parochial committee. They did not speak as he came in.

'Where's the boy?' he said.

They did not answer and for a moment he felt uneasy.

'Ain't nothin' up?' he said.

Then Lily spoke. 'He's in bed,' she said.

'A-bed? What's a' matter?'

She began to raise her voice: 'You ought—'

'Just a minute, Mother,' Walter said. 'I'll say what there is to say.'

They were all silent for a moment. Luke stared. They sat more than ever with a kind of parochial solemnity, all looking at each other, as though not daring to look at him. It was early autumn, there were only faded summer flowers and grasses in the fireplace and the room seemed chilly. At last Walter said:

'I won't have it, Father. Not for nobody. I won't have it.'

'What's a' matter, Walt, what's a' matter?'

'He's responsible—' Lily began.

'Now, Mother, now,' Walter said. He paused a moment. Luke waited, and then Walter said:

'Eddie's been caught in Chelston woods with a snare in his possession.'

'Eh? What, what!'

'Eddie's been caught in Chelston woods,' Walter said. 'By the keepers. With a snare in his pocket.'

'A snare? What happened? What'd they do to the boy?' And then the folly of it struck him. 'What the 'nation was he doing in a wood wi' a snare? A snare ain't no—'

'Never mind about that,' said Walter.

'All right. All right. What'd they do to the boy? Eh?'

'They asked him who he was,' Walter said.

'Ah.'

'Instead of telling them properly, he told them he belonged to you, Luke Bishop.'

'Never? That's a clinker.'

'It hardly made it any better,' Walter said.

The force of the words struck him unexpectedly, so that he could say nothing. He stood staring, wretched, a little bewildered.

'They knew in a minute what that meant,' Walter said.

He had nothing to say.

'Now, Father,' Walter said, 'I won't have it. Not for nobody. It's gone on long enough. You're fond of the boy, but—'

'He'd give him his *head*,' Lily said passionately, 'if he asked for it!'

'Now, Mother, now. Gently.' And then to Luke again: 'You learned him to set the snare, and you see the consequences. Poaching was all very well in your day, but now things are different. We have our own ideas about how Eddie shall grow up.' And then for the first time he half-raised his voice: 'And poaching's not one of them! You understand? You can drop it now, once and for all. I won't have it! Not for nobody. I won't have it! You see?'

'Ah.'

'All right then, that's all.'

'What are they goin' to do to the boy?' Luke said.

'That remains to be seen. It depends on what I can do.'

'God a'mighty, if I catch a sight of them keepers!'

'You'll keep out of it,' Lily said. 'You've done mischief enough already. Do you want it to be all over the town?'

He said nothing. They were all silent too. He was finished, defeated. They were all against him. Then as he stood there, not knowing what to do, Lily and Ellen and Lizzie got up and went out of the room into the front parlour. A moment later Walter got up too, paused as though to say something and then followed them without a word.

Luke went back into the kitchen and sat down without washing. He was full of a stupid, reasonless kind of agony. He could think of nothing but his love for the boy and his own folly.

An hour later Walter came in from the front parlour and found him still sitting there.

'Like the paper, Dad?' he said. He put the newspaper into Luke's hands and then went out again.

Luke went on sitting there for an unconscionable time with the paper unopened in his hands. It was hard for him to read in any case, and already it was too dark for him to see.

Suddenly his mother died. She had been living alone, in an almshouse, almost perversely independent, so cut off from him that for several years she had seemed almost a stranger. Periodically he would send her sacks of potatoes, a hare, a cabbage or two, and at Christmas time some money. She seemed never to have forgiven him for leaving home at the time of the murder, for not explaining where he had been and what he had been doing, and most of all for marrying Lily. It gave her a kind of perverted pleasure to be affronted and distant, to stand on the almshouse doorstep and complain to her neighbour that she was pushed aside, that she was forgotten, that no one wanted her. His sisters had grown more distant still. They had married two brothers, railwaymen, and they lived farther down the line in two raw brick cottages perched high on the railway bank, with nothing but empty fields and unbroken solitude behind them and the incessant thunder of passing expresses in the cutting below. They had endless children, all curiously alike, a little swarthy, whom they brought down to the funeral. Hester's illegitimate boy had married also and had a daughter, dark and sallow like all the rest, so that on the day of the funeral, as they crowded into the little three-roomed almshouse, Luke could not separate one family from another or one generation from another. The railwaymen were there, wearing black suits and squeaky black boots and bowler hats and white flattened-down collars. They were strangers to him, foreign and impersonal. Sal and Hester had grown fat; he could not take his eyes off their podgy legs and hands and drooping bosoms. They contrasted so powerfully with the figures he had once known, the slim, sleepily arrogant figures of his youth very dark and flashily beautiful. They were almost strangers to him also. They spoke a strange accent, evoking no response in him except 'Ah,' or 'Never,' or 'That's a licker.' In the evening, after the funeral was over, and the restrained tight atmosphere had vanished and their black gloves had been pulled off, he left them quarrelling over his mother's belongings, her few chairs and pictures and pillow-slips and the bed in which she had died.

Before the month was out they came back again, with all the children and the two railwaymen in their black suits and starched flattened collars, to quarrel again, but this time not with themselves but with him.

His aunt had died as suddenly as his mother.

There was some money and a will. He had known that for a long time. And when he troubled to think of it at all he had an idea that some of the money, if not all of it, might come to him.

But when, after the funeral, the will was read in the room where he had so often sat with his aunt over a glass of wine in the candle-glowing twilight, and it turned out that not only the money but the house and the books and the furniture and even the wine-glasses and the time-worn antimacassars had been left to him, it was as though he had been surrounded by a pack of chained dogs, all waiting in a state of frenzied and jealous astonishment to tear him to pieces.

It was February, and the barking and frenzied jealousy of his sisters on one side and the thinner yapping and scratching of Lily and his own daughters on the other went on into the summer. He never escaped it. On Saturday or market days Sal or Hester or even both of them would take the cheap excursion to Nenweald in order to see him, to try some new conciliatory scheme on him or more generally some new method of abuse and bitterness. He would find them sitting in the living-room when he arrived home from the field, their flabby haunches squabbling over Lily's rather elegant cane-seated chairs, their cheap violet scents filling the room, the black net veils of the period still drawn over their faces. Or they would come up to the field to him, dressed just the same but a little tired and hot in the black dresses they always wore for the occasion, and stand in the yard or on the land and argue with intermittent abuse while he mixed his pig-swill or hoed his roots, until he was sick of the sound of their squabbling voices and they in turn exhausted all their arguments and took up a chorus of pure abuse.

'Come on, Sal. Don't waste ye breath. I wouldn't waste me breath. If he's so damn mean, let him be. All I can say is it's a good job Alf ain't here. Come on, don't waste ye breath. It goes in one ear and out the other. You might talk to a brick wall. And that your own brother! Your own kin. Christ, come on afore I do summat I s'll wish I hadn't.'

Then, in contrast, there were times when they came accompanied by the railwaymen, always on a Saturday evening, and the two men, agents of conciliation, persuaded him to walk as far as the market place, drop into The Bell, and drink at their expense pints of stout he did not want.

'Go on, Dad, be reasonable. You're comfortable. Share and share alike. It's your own sisters.'

'I tell ye I ain't got it. Not a farden. It ain't settled.'

'I know that. But it will be. And what ye going to do with it all?'

'I don' know.'

'See. That's it. He don' know.'

'He don' know nothing. Don' even know how much it is.'

'No, that's right enough.'

'Well, whatever it is, Dad, share and share alike.'

'You don' wanna be greedy.'

'Have another stout.'

But he would shake his head and finally get up and walk out of the bar, leaving them fuming and with the bill to pay.

On the other side was Lily. In her own mind she arranged the allotment of the money, spent it and built herself a new, higher and more aristocratic place in life long before the lawyers had settled the will and had taken their percentages. Luke was to give up the holding; the old shifty, disreputable way of life was to be wiped out; a new, easier, beyond-reproach kind of existence was to take its place. They would leave the house in which they had always lived and move into the house in the chapel yard. Above all things they must move into the house. It was as though it were next door to Lily's ultimate heaven.

The girls supported their mother; only Walter remained aloof, neutral and unchangeably indifferent. He wanted to create his own world, a world which in turn was to be his son's world. The money did not worry him. He felt no envy. He even had no advice to offer.

Finally Luke drove down into Orcester, ostensibly to market but in reality to see the lawyers. He had never changed his ideas, except momentarily, as to what he would do with the legacy. He had dreamed occasionally of another field, even of a farm, of a cow or two, of a binder. But they were dreams in which he had no belief. They amused him momentarily and then vanished. He returned always, unfailingly, to his original notion.

And when he came back from the lawyers' he took Walter aside, they walked together down the garden path, between the narrow rows of sunflowers and still flowerless chrysanthemums and the tobacco flowers just beginning to open in the twilight. When they reached the hen-coop at the bottom of the garden they paused and looked at the two hens cuddled asleep on the grey-mucked perches. The hens fluttered, shifted along the perches, and then half-opened their eyes. And looking at the hens, as though he were too embarrassed to look at Walter, Luke said:

'I bin to see the lawyers, Walt. I made the money over to you, for Eddie. He'll be able to git to school straight away instead o' waitin'.'

3

The war began and the boy went away to school almost simultaneously. For a long time the war scarcely touched Luke; but the departure of the boy affected him profoundly. Without him he felt lost. He suffered from an illusion that he would never see him again. The weeks between the beginning of the school term and its end became weeks of imprisonment, a wretched routine of dark and daylight which even the war did nothing to lighten or change. Lily became swept up in a wave of patriotic romance, the girls with her, and Walter in a storm of industry, executing vast orders for boots for the Russian army. Men began to be taken away from the town and the land, and gradually a strange silence and solitude settled over the field. The big gangs of hoers or ditchers shrivelled to one or two, and then became replaced by women or prisoners of war. The prisoners marched to work in the morning and away again in the evening in little squads under an armed guard, their grey uniforms more desolate than the winter land itself. Meeting them in the early mornings or the twilight Luke would stare at them and they would stare in return, but no one would speak. He would have liked to speak. He felt a lack of communication. He began to work again in the old speechless solitude, speaking to no one from morning till evening, talking to himself, always thinking of the boy.

And gradually he felt that he must do something to break or loosen the tension of solitude. He began to look for extra work to occupy him, war-work, something patriotic. Then he thought of cutting his hedges, the big twenty-foot hawthorn hedges that bordered his field and had never been cut for perhaps thirty years. And when he began to split and lay the boughs he saw new views; it gave him momentarily a fresh outlook; it seemed to let in a fresh flood of daylight. The field adjoining his own sloped away sharply, towards a stream. Along the hedges, at intervals, there were young spruces. He had scarcely noticed them before. One evening he stood looking at them. Their branches were black and delicate against the raw winter sky. He stood still, silent. And presently, at the foot of the field, rabbits began to come out quietly to feed, making brown bunches in the grass. He stood transfixed. More and more rabbits appeared, more rabbits than he had seen for a long time. They made a living, quiet colony across the field. He stood there watching until it was almost too dark to see, marvelling softly to himself, the rabbits

174

feeding and playing almost tamely all the time about the darkening grass.

He went home, thought about it, and finally decided to buy some nets. His father had always bought nets from a little rope and twine shop near the river wharf. The shop had been kept by a man named Booth. Bishop and Booth had transacted in a kind of crude code language: cobwebs were nets, pussies were rabbits. Luke went down to the wharf. The shop, with the name Booth painted on it, was still there, with the same odd coils of rope and jute as of old lying among out-of-date playbills in the window. It was evening and the window-gas, turned down, was burning green. Luke went in. A fat man in shirt-sleeves came into the shop. He was bald-headed and screwed up his nose and eyes as he looked at Luke. He was Booth's son. Luke saw the likeness clearly. They looked at each other for a moment and then Luke said:

'Any cobwebs?'

Booth screwed up his face as he came from behind the counter to look more closely at Luke.

'Christ Jesus, it's Bish, ain't it?'

'Ah.'

'Huh, cobwebs.' He spoke in a husky, suppressed voice. 'Ain't heard that word for thirty year.' He stood there scratching his chin with the back of one hand. 'What y' going to do, catch Germans?'

'Ah.'

'All the Germans you catch, I'll buy. Skin an' all. Cash.'

'That's a deal.'

'Want ferrets, too?'

It was the beginning of a transaction which lasted throughout the war. It was as though he had been switched back into the old life. At first he had some doubts. He would have to work single-handed. He had never done that. Then he had misgivings about himself. It was years since he had touched a net, and he could not bear the thought of working clumsily or badly. But whenever he thought of the rabbits, in quiet colonies stretching across the field, he could bear still less the thought of not working at all. Then he mistrusted Booth. He fretted over the fear of some duplicity.

And on the first night he was nervous with misgivings and excitement. Things for some reason were not right. His footsteps seemed loud and harsh in the dead winter grass, the ferrets were restless in his pocket, the stars were curiously bright. He discovered he was trembling. He kept working over and over in his mind the routine of spreading and pegging the nets, introducing the ferrets, waiting for the first rabbit. He felt that he had forgotten something. He kept trying to remember what it was, and while he was still trying to remember what it was he began to execute the first movement of opening the nets, pegging them, pausing in alert and mechanical attitudes of listening. For a moment or two it was all unconscious. He had the net outspread and the first peg driven in the earth before he came to himself, aroused by the sudden damp proximity of the earth, the smell of bruised grass, the feel of it on his hands. And he stood astonished by his own lightness and quickness, by the ease with which it had all come back to him. It was a masterpiece, a licker. His fears began to recede and become meaningless. He was working with great rapidity. On the land he was inclined to be a slow worker, deliberate. He moved about the nets with amazing agility and silence, working without thinking, his movements instinctive. It was not until he had the net laid and the ferret in his hands that he paused at all. He had the ferret-string tied to his leg. He listened for one moment before releasing the ferret into the burrow. The night was very quiet; there was not even the sound of a distant train. He let go the ferret and waited. The silence seemed to expand into the darkness in infinite circles, like rings on a pool. Then it was broken by a sudden rush and struggle almost under his hands, the wild struggle of the first rabbit escaping into the imprisonment of the net. In a moment he had the rabbit in his hands. Then he felt the head-bone hard on his hands as he struck it. And then for a single second a running of excitement through his blood before the wild rush and struggle began in the net again.

After that, except when the nights were too light and the weather treacherous, he worked all through the successive winters of the war. After the exhilaration of the first night was over he lapsed for a little while into the old state of apprehension. He took the first rabbits down to Booth under a load of cauliflowers. And as he drove through the streets of the town he could see all sorts of suspicions in the eyes of police and soldiers. But gradually it passed. He was reading into the faces of other people his own suspicions. When his own suspicions had vanished he saw that he feared nobody and suspected nobody. He began to see also that no one troubled about him or the land or the poaching of rabbits any longer. Beside the war they were insignificant things. And like the emptiness of the land itself that indifference was providential. The land's emptiness never ceased to amaze him. No keepers, only solitary men working in twenty-acre fields and the little forlorn squads of prisoners. On Sundays he would walk about the land or by the river in simple amazement at the deserted quietness. The river-keepers had long since gone, and the new tanneries, built up on the escarpment and working at hysterical pressure that only ceased on Sundays, were poisoning the stream with a greenish milky chemical overflow. He would listen for the plop of fish in vain. And on the land, in woods where he had seen keepers in squads patrolling the ridings at nesting-time, there was the same unearthly desolation and desertion. He would see the pheasant coops wind-wrecked and nettle-choked in ridings that were choked up themselves or ploughed into alleys of mud by government timber-wagons. He stood amazed at the great numbers of the predatory birds and animals, the magpies haunting the woods in black and white companies, the stoats and weasels foraging the hedge-sides in little armies. He walked in woods and coverts where he had scarcely ever dared to walk before except by night. And he continued all the time with the poaching, working first the warren in the field edging his own, then farther afield, then still farther, until he had a little circle of grounds. He existed in a state of almost constant secretive exhilaration. It was like a return to drinking after some long and deadly period of starved sobriety.

It was the poaching also that saved him from ultimate wretchedness which he felt while the boy was at school. But when the boy came home on holiday it receded. It became instantly a secondary thing.

When Eddie came home for his second holiday he wore long trousers, he seemed almost to have grown up. He was anxious to be a runner. He was built lightly and he moved easily. Luke tried him along the road on an early spring morning. Eddie, in his flimsy shorts and vest, came along the road like a feather. Luke remembered Reeves, just as thin and light. Eddie moved like him. But back in the hut, as he towelled and rubbed him down, Luke was critical.

'Ye knees ain't up. They're flabby. Ye got to bring 'em up. Hit your chin with 'em. See that? And don't wave your arms about. You run wi' your legs, not your arms. And how d'ye breathe? Show me.'

And gradually he began to shape the boy. And again it was like old days, out with Reeves and his father in the quiet early mornings of the other century. It renewed his exhilaration. So that he forgot his extreme loneliness.

Then the boy wanted to learn boxing. 'Now you're talking,' Luke said. 'Running and boxing go together. Know that? If one fails, you got t'other. If you don't catch a man hard enough you can run. Folks 'll tell you as it's on'y cowards as run away. Don't you believe it. I ran away anew times myself and I know. I shouldn't be here now if I hadn't run.'

They sparred in a quiet corner behind the straw stacks. Luke would flat-hand the boy, moving casually, making him miss. The boy was very quick, coming in with light electric punches. 'That's it. Hit, stop, jab and get away. You won't better that. And look at me. *Look* at me. Look at my eyes. You're looking at Chelston church steeple. It's no good, it's no good. You won't hit me 'ithout you look at me.'

For both of them it was a wonderful time. They were each other's counterparts. The boy spent all his time in the field and Luke all his time thinking of him and for him. When the boy boxed or ran badly Luke nursed him, cajoled him. 'You're all right. But what's your trainin' for? No use going wild. I boxed afore you were born.' Or if the boy were cocky: 'Ah, you're all right. Passable. But I could ha' knocked flies off you. You're only playing. I *had* to run. And fight, too.'

It was only when the school term began again that the tension of happiness was broken for them both and Luke was plunged back again into the war, the solitude of the deserted fields, the nightly poaching and the eternal suffering expectation of the boy's return. The boy wrote him letters, relating his running exploits. He could never write back. And they kept up a distant worship of each other.

By the end of the war Luke was a man of almost sixty. He walked more than ever with a stoop, so that he looked older. His skin, which hung on his bones like thick loose leather, seemed to be stained with a colour somewhere between earth and sunlight. He went about with an air of independent secrecy, taking little or no part in the hysterical war-life. He could only read the papers with spectacles. He was a man apart. In addition to the smell of animal muck and earth, which Lily said hung about him perpetually, there was a faint odour of skinned rabbits. His still blew his nose without a handkerchief and he still preferred a muffler to a collar. His black hair was turning a greyish-white and his legs were stiff when he first got up in the dark mornings.

4

The primroses were fully out in the sparse copses and the white violets on the moist ditch-sides as Luke and Eddie walked across the ridge above Tichmarsh on the last after-

noon of April in 1920. In the morning the boy was to go back
to school for his last term. At the end of that term he would sit
for his examinations and on the result of them depended his
future.

'I may go to the University,' he said.

'University? College like? What d'ye reckon to do there?'

'Learn a bit more.'

'French and like that?'

'H'm.'

'What's the use of them foreign lingoes?'

They went slowly across the ridge, on the footpath running by the woods, discussing it all. It was soft weather, the
primroses were warm and gave up their scent. At the top of
the ridge Luke paused and turned and looked over the
hollow. The day was sunny and cloudy, there was an everlasting race of light and shadow across the land, the young
wheat-fields lightened and darkened. The light was wonderfully clear, making odd spires and yellow sallow trees and
men working on the field slopes visible at a great distance.
Luke began to point out the landmarks. The pub where he
had so often gone with his father shone white and dark in the
hollow, like a bird-splash. He had never been in for years.
Beyond it he could see the path coming down the slope. The
same solitary ash trees marked out the road above it.

'God a'mighty, times I've been across there in the dark.
Like as many sovereigns. See that gate? Bottom o' that
wheat-field, near the sloe bushes? The old dad belted a
keeper there once. Laid him out.' He looked across the land,
pointing, falling into reminiscence. 'We used to cut across the
top there. Then down through the gate. Then in the pub.
Then up o' this side.' He was chewing a primrose stalk and
he had one hand stuck in his belt. Suddenly he let the stalk
fall. He could see the field where the hen-woman had cried
out at him on the afternoon of Baron's murder. And suddenly
instead of the sunlight he could see the snow, Baron lying
dead in the ditch, and he himself running up the field. 'Rum

goings on. Fool's bits we used to do.' He began to walk on again. 'Licker to me how we ever got away.'

'Didn't you ever get copped?'

'No. Never. I could *run*. That's what I tell you. It's no use if you can't run.'

They walked on by the woodside. The wood silence was broken only by their own voices, the clapping together of boughs in the wind and the dainty pattering of odd birds among the dead leaves. The land was quiet, but the old war-time silence had gone, like the squad of prisoners and the women land-workers. There was a curious sense of uneasiness instead. Keepers were about, people watching, the trespassing notices were being repainted. Luke could feel it wherever he went. It made him more wary, less sure of himself on the nightly poaching jaunts. But up on the ridge, pointing out the old landmarks to the boy, going off into memory, he forgot it for a while.

Almost at the end of the wood he stopped to listen to a sudden cry. The boy stopped also. The cry, coming from the wood, was fitful and piercing, a little agonized shriek of animal terror.

Luke rushed to the wood fence. 'Ah, he's got him, he's nailed him. It's a done-go.' He paused. And then:

'A rabbit. A stoat. Can you twig him? Eh? Can you twig him?' They were leaning together over the wood fence, searching the brown floor of leaves. And suddenly they saw the snaky motions of the stoat, startled, as it retreated into the wood, leaving the rabbit hunched against the earth in its paralysed condition of dying and terror.

Luke began to climb the fence. 'He's ourn,' he kept saying. 'He's ourn.' The boy followed him. The rabbit was still crying, but more quietly. It skulked against the earth flattened and motionless, paralysed, not even moving as Luke ran forward to seize it. It gave its only struggles as he picked it up, a sudden convulsive start just before he struck it behind the neck and then another, lengthening out, as it died.

When the boy came up, Luke laid the rabbit's head in one hand, holding its feet with the other, and began to explain about the stoat bite. 'See it? No bigger'n a shilling. You'll hear folks say a stoat mesmerizes a rabbit. It don't. It paralyses it. That's why she couldn't move. See?' There were odd smears of blood on his hands. He began to put the rabbit into his pocket.

Suddenly he stopped. Then he began to speak rapidly, in alarm.

Someone was coming down the wood path.

'Christ, run, run! Git on with it! Run!'

'What's up?'

'Run, I tell you. Christ, run! A keeper!'

The boy, turning, saw the keeper coming at a low half-running stride under the trees. He was shouting. The boy began to scramble over the fence. Luke was still putting the rabbit in his pocket. He seemed to be moving clumsily, as though the rabbit were too big for his pocket, and he was smearing the blood on his coat and his hands. The keeper was not more than twenty yeards away when he finally pocketed the rabbit and began to run. He was still calling to the boy, who was running down the field, as he began to climb the fence.

He was still climbing the fence when the keeper leapt at him. He leapt full on him like an animal. The sheer weight of his body dragged Luke down. He staggered backwards, the keeper half-pulling him. Luke tried to wrench himself free, the two falling together. He was on his feet again quickly and as the keeper leapt to his feet also he swung his left arm and hit him full in the face. The keeper roared. He was a young man, tall, with a handsome brown moustache and high red cheek-bones, and in the second before he hit him Luke was reminded of Baron. Then he went at him again. The keeper stood still, waiting. Luke felt a mad desire to hit him full in the mouth. He would wipe the moustache off his face. He swung his arm. In a second he felt the bone of the keeper's mouth on his knuckles and then a single instant of the old exhilaration before the keeper hit him in return.

The blow hit him in the chest, above the heart. The heart seemed at once to go dead. He could not breathe. The keeper came at him again madly, hitting him wildly on the head and face. Luke tried to cover himself. He pressed himself against the keeper until his breath returned. The keeper pushed him away with both hands and then began to smash him, forcing him backwards, hitting him anywhere.

Luke staggered about a little and then fell. Then, as he tried to rise, the keeper fell flat on top of him. He fell like a tree. He pinned his neck against the earth with one hand and then began to hit with the other. Luke tried to lift his knees and push him away. It was almost the last thing he remembered. The keeper began to hit him with such fury that he had the impression that all the keepers he had ever known were hitting him. Then all the trees in the wood seemed to be falling down. After that all he remembered was the keeper hitting and kicking him, like a maniac, as he lay on the ground and covered his face with his hands.

CHAPTER III

I

THE day they let him out of prison at Orcester he walked home to Nenweald by the river, along the towpath. It was early August: the wheat-fields on the long valley slopes were half-cut, half-standing, yellowish-white expanses broken by the dark aisles of shocks and the moving binders. But he felt that the summer was over. It was a dull day, with a little fretting wind coming down the river, ruffling and turning over the willow-leaves, so that they shone suddenly white at intervals before going dull again. The water was lightless except where the wind caught it and stirred up a series of feathery ripples that it carried upstream like little shoals of silver leaves. He walked quietly, not hurrying, sitting to rest on the nailed-up towpath gates. He was thinking all the time that he had nothing to hurry for.

As he left the path and went over the bridge and up the meadow lane the hooters and sirens were beginning to blow in the town for the dinner hour. It would be half-past twelve. The sounds lasted for half a minute and then were dead. He could feel the silence hanging over the valley and the town as though it were something tangible. It was as though the whole place and the whole countryside as far as he could see had gone suddenly lifeless. Up on the slopes the binders had come to a standstill simultaneously. The quietness was complete except for the wind turning over the willow leaves and whinning now and then in the harsh thorns of the sloe trees. He walked on the cow ridges. They had been baked like stone by the summer. He wondered what sort of summer it had been. He kept stopping to look at the fields of uncut wheat or barley lying on either side of the lane, trying to judge. After a moment of looking at the length of the straw or the droop of the ears he would go off into a kind of momentary trance, not thinking, his face almost stupefied. He looked as though lost in thought, but his mind was empty. He was conscious of nothing but the noon silence over the town and the land.

It was the silence which aroused him at last. It made him begin to walk faster than he had walked all morning. He wanted to be in the town before the hooters began again and the silence was broken, and he hurried up the lane and under the walnut tree and into the street without pausing again.

The town was deserted. The late summer noon silence was complete. He met no one except odd factory hands having long distances to go, and nothing else moved except the street trees fluttering and little spirals and whirlwinds of summer dust rising and settling at street corners. He saw no one he knew. He was used to that. He had seen no one he knew, except Lily, for three months. And Lily he had seen only for ten minutes on a prison visiting day. She had come to ask his decision on a question of the field. The owner, the son of the baker from whom he had begun to rent it years before, wished to terminate the agreement. He would offer some compensation for the standing crops and the buildings. Walter suggested fifty pounds. But they wanted to be fair; not to do anything unless Luke himself agreed. All the time she talked he was not listening. He sat staring at his hands. Her voice was like a music-roll playing a mechanical tune, incapable of a mistake. It went on coldly and perfectly until the tune was finished. When it was finished he still sat there staring at his hands, saying nothing. 'Well, what do you say?' she said. Then he looked up. 'Where's the boy?' he said. She did not answer. Then he noticed a curious thing. Lily was in black. His heart came up into his throat in terror. 'What y're in black for?' he demanded. 'Eh?' She said nothing. 'The boy's all right, ain't he?' She moistened her lips with her tongue. 'Oh, yes, he's all right.' He looked her up and down. 'Then what y're in black for?' She was looking away from him. 'I thought it was suitable.' He looked at her with a kind of repressed contempt. 'I ain't dead yet,' he said. He had scarcely spoken before she was crying, dabbing her face with her screwed-up handkerchief, her lips convulsed as she tried to suppress her tears. Then she spoke as she cried. 'All the trouble I've had with you and now you speak like that.' He let her go on, not troubling, feeling nothing for her, not saying another word until he bade her good-bye. That was all he had seen of her and her world since the morning the magistrate had said, reciting his words almost as Lily had recited hers: 'This class of offence is very much on the increase. We can't have people indiscriminately trespassing on preserves and assaulting the keepers. Property has to be protected.' And after Lily's visit there was a letter from Walter. It was written in Walter's business language. 'The lease of the field has been terminated by mutual agreement. We have received forty-five pounds compensation, and this sum is in mother's safekeeping.' There was a postscript about the boy: 'Eddie is at school. You will understand what we feel about his future.'

He was thinking of it all in odd snatches as he went up the street and across the Square in the midday silence. Behind the Square, in the chapel yard, the air seemed quieter than ever. He went to the door of his aunt's old house and knocked and then waited. Nothing happened. He waited a little longer. Then he saw a note fixed to the lintel with a drawing pin:

'No milk.'

Underneath that, in Lily's new script writing, was a second notice:

'No bread.'

He walked slowly down the yard, into the street again, and then across the Square. He was moving with the same air as he had looked at the cornfields, in a kind of trance, vacantly. But now he was thinking. He was trying to consider what he should do, where he should go. And for a moment or two he could not make up his mind. He stood under the chestnut trees, thinking. Then as he stood there the church clock struck a quarter-past one and he became conscious of a breaking in the silence about the streets, the murmur of returning feet and voices. He could see here and there the flap of leather-stained aprons in the little summer wind. There was still a silence, but it was receding. A wave of noises, feet and voices and bicycles and cars and carts and then the preliminary sirens, was advancing.

It almost caught him up as he left the Square and went through the churchyard and over the railway bridge towards the fields. He walked more quickly. It had occurred to him that he might look at the field. It seemed to him, even though it was no longer his, still very much a part of him, a fixed and unchangeable association. He wanted to look at it, to see what had happened to it, who had taken it after him.

Over the railway bridge he paused to stare in astonishment. Great changes were in progress. It was as though he had come back to a new world. The fields that for as long as he could remember had come down to the railway fence were no longer fields. They were changed and were being changed into streets. Pink and blue rows of new workmen's dwelling-houses were rising in all directions to the east and north. Gangs of labourers were beginning to work again after the dinner hour. The dust blew off the unpaved streets in sudden sandy clouds, and he could smell the fresh clay that was being dug up from the new foundations.

He could not find the footpath. At all other times he had taken a short cut across the fields, through a spinney, and so to his own field. Now he could not find the path. He wandered about half-lost trying to find the path, going up and down the half-finished streets, coming out at last on the road just below the gate of the field.

At the gate he stopped and looked. Changes were beginning to take place in the field also. The buildings that he and Walter had put up had been taken down. Nothing remained. He could see the strawed square where the pig-sties had stood, the dung-stained area of the stables and the hen-house. The straw stack had been taken away. Nothing remained of the yard except the space of summer-baked earth bright with pink and white convolvulus flowers, tufts of camomile, and a few wind-broken stalks of the sun-flowers Lily had planted many years ago.

But beyond the yard it seemed as if the field had never been touched. White strips of wheat and barley and the darker interplantings of roots and potatoes still remained, the corn combed across by the perpetual little wind running up the field. The sudden familiarity of it all was like a pain. He stood again in a trance, staring, once again thinking of nothing. All his thoughts were compressed and concentrated into a single point of suffering, something he could not explain or analyse or understand.

Then as he stood there staring he became aware of two figures in the field. Two young men had been sitting under the hedge just below him, eating their lunch. Now they were moving out into the field. They were carrying what looked to him like a kind of tripod. They were trying to find a level standing place for it among the potatoes. They would set up the tripod and then something would be wrong and they would move to another place, one carrying the tripod, like a man with a camera, the other rolls of paper, a pole and a book or two. Finally, unable to find a place among the potatoes, they moved back to the cart track that ran along the hedge by the roadside. They stood just below Luke and set up the tripod and then squinted through it, making preliminary sights.

He watched them. For a moment he was taken out of himself. He was interested in what they were doing, and slightly perplexed. He could not understand the tripod.

Then the young men saw him looking. They looked at him and nodded and then said, 'Good afternoon.'

'How do?' he said.

Presently one young man walked away down the field, the other looked through the instrument on the tripod, and they began to take sights again. The man down the field set up the pole, and the other, taking the sight, made signs with his arms, like a soldier signalling. They made notes and then moved again, coming nearer the gate.

He felt suddenly that he wanted to speak. He waited until the young man had fixed the tripod and then said:

'What y'up to?'

'Surveying.'

'Ah. Thought you were taking pictures.'

The young man took a sight and spoke in a preoccupied kind of voice while still squinting. 'Not much to take pictures of here. No. We're surveying.'

'What's that for?'

'Houses. New road.'

'Ah.'

The young man made signals and seemed more than ever preoccupied, and there was a silence. Then he relaxed, the second man began to walk up the field, and Luke said:

'What's the idea o' the telescope?'

The young man was still laughing when his friend came up. 'He wants to know what the idea of the telescope is?' he said.

'Let him have a look.'

'Come and have a look,' the other said.

Almost mechanically Luke unfastened the gate and went into the field. He stood with his arms loose at his side, embarrassed.

'Shut one eye and look through there.'

He went up to the tripod and squinted through the sight, but he could see nothing except the dim glassy greens and yellows that he knew must be the end of the field. It was as though he were seeing something in a crystal or in water.

'See anything?'

'It ain't very clear.'

'Half a minute.' The young man looked through the sight himself, adjusted it, and then said: 'I forgot. Now try.'

Luke squinted his eye once more and looked through the sight, earnestly, but he could see nothing again except that vague and as though melted pattern of green and gold, as if the wheat and the grass had turned to water and the land were being dissolved before his eyes.

'See anything now?'

He shook his head and then gave it up.

'You're not used to it,' the young man said.

'My eyes ain't very good.'

He began to walk back to the gate as soon as he had spoken, and the young men were comparing notes in their books before he had shut the gate and had reached the road.

He stood watching them for a moment while he fastened the gate-hook. But they were engrossed. They seemed to have forgotten him, and finally he began to walk away down the road.

All the way back he could see the blue roofs of the new streets shining dully in the sunless air, and every now and then he could see also a cloud of dust caught by the wind and lifted up and carried along in a brief whirlwind over the still untouched fields, like a cloud of sand-coloured seed. Then he would turn and stand for a moment and watch the young men in the field. They were still busy, holding the pole, still looking through the instrument and signalling to each other as though in some strange language in another world. Every time he paused he would wait a little longer, and each time he went on again he walked more slowly than before.

It was only then beginning to occur to him fully that he had nowhere to go.

GENERAL FICTION

SPORTS

FOOTBALL

BOXING

GOLF

SEND TODAY!

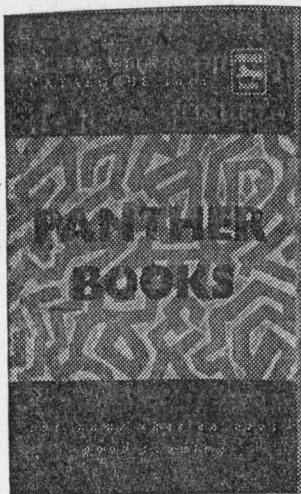

*Free
of
charge*

*Colourful
and
profusely
illustrated*

Send your name and address, and you will receive a copy of
a colourful and profusely illustrated brochure giving full
details of our forthcoming books.

Why not be on our Mailing List?

Panther books consist of a varied range of titles carefully chosen
from the lists of British and American publishers. They include
War books, Novels, Westerns, Thrillers, Science-fiction and Books-
of-the-Films. Ask your bookseller for the latest Panther releases.

*If you have any difficulty in obtaining supplies, copies
can be obtained (include 3d. postage per book) from :*

**Dept. 914, Panther Books, 108 Brompton Road,
Knightsbridge, London, S.W.3.**